Kim Larabee

BEHIND
The Mask

Kim Larabee

BEHIND
The Mask

Boston • Alyson Publications, Inc.

Copyright © 1989 by Kim Larabee. All rights reserved.
Typeset and printed in the United States of America.
Cover art copyright © 1989 by Catherine Hopkins.

Published as a trade paperback original by
Alyson Publications
40 Plympton Street
Boston, Massachusetts 02118

Distributed in the U.K. by GMP Publishers,
PO Box 247, London, N17 9QR, England.

First U.S. edition: June, 1989

ISBN 1-55583-151-6
LC 88-083327

All characters in this book are fictitious.
Any resemblance to real persons, living or dead,
is strictly coincidental.

Behind the Mask
editor: Sasha Alyson
production and design: Wayne Curtis
proofreading: Tina Portillo
printing: McNaughton & Gunn
Lithographers

*This book is dedicated to Bea,
without whom it would never
have been written.*

*And special thanks to Anne,
who always believed
it could be better*

Kim Larabee

BEHIND
The Mask

One

The mist swirled around the silhouetted figure on the hill. The moonlight traced the hazy outline, and here and there gleamed harshly off the bits of silver. For a moment one could discern a rider and horse standing idly, and then the cantankerous moon would once more slip behind the foreboding clouds. The horse stamped impatiently, dispelling the idea of idleness and replacing it with a sense of barely controlled excitement. The rider laid a gloved hand against the dark neck and murmured soft noises. The horse tipped his ears back to listen, cocking one hip as he relaxed. The rider snuggled deeper into his cloak and pulled his hat farther down over his forehead, creating an ominous figure, totally and completely black, except for the silver of bit and stirrup. The rider reached into his pockets and checked his pistols once more. Everything had to be perfect.

The horse pricked his ears forward, bringing the rider to sudden attention. Far off down the road the rumbling of a heavy coach could be heard. The rider smiled. The coachman was springing his horses in order to clear the woods quickly, afraid of highwaymen. The rider's smile deepened into a grin, his teeth gleaming in the darkness. Quickly he pulled out the two pistols and cautiously cocked them. The horse began to dance beneath him, and the rider steadied him with voice and knee. Both were quiet now, and rigidly alert.

The coach drew abreast, and the horse sprang forward to the road. The report of the pistol startled the coach horses and sent them bolting to the other side of the road. Desperately, the coachman tried to pull them up, causing one horse to rear suddenly. In the resulting confusion all four horses managed to get hopelessly tangled in their traces, holding the coachman's undivided attention.

The rider dropped the still-smoking pistol into a pocket with a sincere prayer that it would not burn his new cloak, and urged his horse to the side of the coach. In one fluid motion he leaned over and jerked the door open, allowing a clear view of his masked face to the occupant within. The white gleam of his grin was sinister as he thrust the remaining pistol at the passenger inside — a merchant, no less. The grin broadened, but lost none of its wickedness.

"Step down, sir," the rich, deep voice of the rider commanded. The glitter of the steely eyes behind the mask brooked no refusal.

The merchant climbed awkwardly out of the coach, vainly trying to pull his overcoat over the gold watch chain at his waist.

"Come, sir, hand over your purse. Certainly you must know this is a robbery!"

"You damned swine," the merchant hissed in response as he plunged a hand into his pocket. "All you get is this!" The pistol in his hand fired as he spoke, the bullet passing cleanly through the folds of the rider's cloak.

"I grow tired of you, little man," said the rider through gritted teeth. He placed the pistol against the merchant's temple. "Your purse, now!"

The merchant brought forth a heavy purse, and was quickly relieved of it. The gold watch, and the rings adorning his fingers followed.

The rider tipped his hat and wheeled his horse into the woods. The coachman, infuriated at being made so helpless by the highwayman, made an impulsive dive towards his musket. The horses, feeling the sudden release of the reins, began to plunge and rear, making the firing of the musket impossible. The coachman's curses rang out loudly and were answered by the echo of laughter from deep within the trees.

† † † † †

A dark figure slipped up the path from the stables to a side door. Furtively, it lifted the latch and stepped inside. A sudden blaze of light caused Magdalena to draw breath sharply. She expelled slowly as her eyes adjusted to the bright glow of the candle.

"My god, Marta, are you trying to scare me to death? Is everyone abed?"

"Aye, Miss Maddie. It was an easy night. Now, upstairs with you, and to bed. It'll be light soon enough."

"All right, Marta. Just let me lock this away in the library, and I'll follow you up."

Maddie watched Marta gracefully sway away down the hall and derisively rested her hands on her own boyishly slim hips. "Just as well," she thought with a sigh, and followed Marta down the hall in her own, straightforward way.

She gently turned the latch to the library. Entering, she felt for the taper Marta always left on the table by the door. Her eyes narrowed as the candle was lit, and she made her way over to the huge desk. The folds of her long black cloak stirred as she withdrew a heavy purse from her belt. She eased into a chair and spilled the treasure on the desk. A smile chased across her face as she counted. It had been an exciting night. Of course she regretted the hole in her cloak. It meant it would have to be replaced even though it was new. Hard to explain a bullet hole in the shoulder, though.

Maddie chuckled. "Hard to explain the whole outfit," she thought as she stretched her black-panted and -booted legs in front of her. What a scandal! Her face split into a wide grin as she thought of stern Aunt Agatha's face; if her aunt could see her now! "Not really so funny," she thought, the grin quickly fading from her face.

Hurriedly she dug the strongbox out of the drawer and placed the money in it. Moving quickly now, she replaced the box and strode towards the door. The candle was extinguished and carefully replaced. The door closed quietly behind her.

Marta opened the door to her as she reached her room.

"Hurry now, will you? All we need is for your aunt's maid to see you like that! Sit. Let me pull those boots off."

Maddie smiled indulgently as her maid continued to fuss and tug at her. As if they hadn't been through this a thousand times! Marta would always fuss, no matter how she enjoyed the danger. In a matter of minutes Maddie was bundled into bed, the incriminating clothes stashed away in the false floor of the wardrobe.

"Thank you, Marta," Maddie called sleepily from her bed. "You'll have to fence the rings right away. Oh, and I need a new cloak — a bullet hole this time." She chuckled huskily at Marta's whispered and exasperated scolding as the maid quietly let herself out of the room.

† † † † †

12

Marta was still scolding as she pulled back the curtains the next morning. Bustling briskly, she bundled Maddie out of bed and into a morning dress. Maddie was still half asleep as Marta sat her down at the dressing table and went to work on her hair.

"Oh, Marta! What an awful dress!" Maddie exclaimed as Marta was pushing her towards the door. "It's much too young for me," she said, looking at the puffed sleeves in disgust. "I should never let you pick out my clothes in the morning! Where did you dig this out from? I know *I* never bought it!"

"Your aunt picked it out. It was delivered yesterday with her ball dress for tonight. She was quite certain you would want to wear it this morning." Marta's voice was full of unspoken meaning.

"Oh no!" said Maddie in despair. "Again?"

Marta dropped a solemn nod, and with gentle pressure propelled Maddie to the door.

Maddie clutched the doorway. "Can't I have a headache, Marta?" she asked despairingly.

Shaking her head, Marta gave Maddie a firm thrust into the hall. With one wry look backward, Maddie slowly made her way to the stair. Heaving a heavy sigh, she squared her shoulders and moved gracefully down the stairs.

Tipping her head up at a jaunty angle, Maddie entered the breakfast room and politely bade her aunt good morning. Lady Elverton smiled approvingly at Maddie, and with a regal nod returned the greeting.

"You're looking very fine this morning, Maddie."

Maddie hid her derisive look by turning her attention to the breakfast laid before her. "Thank you, Aunt," she mumbled.

"Maddie, I've granted Lord Edmund permission to call this morning. I hope that this time you'll refrain from discussing horse flesh. It is simply not done, my dear."

"But Aunt, it's the only subject Lord Edmund is knowledgeable about! Certainly, a lady should put a gentleman at ease?"

"He would be more relaxed if you would refrain from staring at him in that devastating way. Really, dear, you can't will intelligent phrases out of him. You must coax him, dear, and avoid correcting him. After all, at five and twenty you are quite on the shelf. You should be grateful that a man of the earl's standing is interested. Be careful child, or you will have a very lonely spinster's life."

"Yes, Aunt Agatha," answered Maddie softly, and in despair she began to wonder if she was some kind of freak. Suitors had passed through her life, sometimes appealing to her mind, and sometimes to her sense of humour. None had ever attracted her heart, or given her the slightest urge to spend her life with them. And yet, it wasn't that she wanted to be alone.

A very sad sigh escaped Maddie, and her aunt's face softened in love and concern for a moment. In that moment there was a strong feeling of unity and kinship, but the mood and the look were abruptly erased as Maddie moved to lift her eyes to her aunt's face.

"I'm sorry, Aunt. I don't mean to be difficult. I guess I just don't appreciate the Earl of Alvon's finer qualities."

Aunt Agatha simply nodded, and the rest of the meal was spent talking of the party they were attending that night.

† † † † †

The ladies had just retired to their drawing room when Lord Edmund arrived. His tall, loose-limbed frame made him appear awkward as he bowed over Aunt Agatha's hand. His wide brown eyes smiled shyly at Maddie as he greeted her, causing Maddie to experience a rush of sympathy for her awkward suitor. In a moment of empathy, she greeted Lord Edmund more warmly than she had intended, causing the young man to experience a sudden rush of emotion. He gave her hand a meaningful squeeze and sat next to her on the couch. Maddie's heart sank into her stomach at the adoring look on his face.

"Are you attending the marchioness's ball tonight, Lord Edmund?" enquired Lady Elverton in formal tones.

"I had planned to attend. I was hoping to coax you and Miss Elverton into allowing me to escort you there this evening." The earl's polite tones failed to hide the eagerness in his voice.

"That would be excellent, Lord Edmund. It's comforting to have a male presence at these crushes."

Maddie could barely keep her lips from curling into a sneer. How many times had she heard these same inane sentences played and replayed? Everybody moving carefully through the same script, over and over again. She almost laughed at the thought of changing the whole act. What if she simply blurted out that she didn't care to attend any tragically boring ball with a moron like Eddie-dear, as she was simply too exhausted after holding up a coach last night? If only it wouldn't result in her being locked up in Bedlam! Her lips tipped slightly upward.

"Miss Elverton?" There was Lord Edmund's voice recalling her to reality. She realized that she had missed the whole train of the conversation, and stared blankly at Lord Edmund in hopes of discovering a clue to the gist. However, Lord Edmund's face held nothing but agonizing, breathless hope mixed with despair.

"Lord Edmund is requesting a dance, Magdalena." Lady Elverton's voice cut through the awkward moment. "Surely you can remember whether the waltz is free for the earl?"

Maddie flashed a grateful smile at her aunt. "I'm sorry, my lord, that my memory is so wanting. I'm sure that I have no partner for that dance. Shall I put your name on my card?"

Lord Edmund nodded eagerly, and was so moved by Maddie's magnitude that he ventured to ask her to go for a drive with him this morning. Luckily for Maddie, Viscount Perry had stolen the march on the earl, and Maddie was able to gracefully decline.

The Earl of Alvon went away disappointed, but in no way cast down. The promise of the coming ball held his attention like a charm. Certainly Magdalena was no longer indifferent to him, just shy. Tonight he would woo her in force.

Maddie heaved a sigh of relief, excused herself to her aunt, and made her way up to her room to change into a walking dress for her drive with the viscount.

The viscount had just entered as Maddie descended the stairs. He looked up at her as he pulled off his gloves, and greeted her with a hearty "Hello there, Maddie! You're looking mighty fine, my dear!" much to the severe disapproval of the very proper butler attending him. The same butler suffered a further blow to his sense of propriety as the viscount continued, "Hurry Maddie. Let's slip out of here before that old bat gets her claws in me. It's too fine a day to be prosing over teacups!"

Maddie, far from being shocked by his familiar form of address, was so moved that she had to cover her mouth with her hand to conceal the laughter obviously displayed there. She was totally unaware of the devastating effect of her dancing, laughing grey eyes, invitingly peering out from under a fringe of dusky locks. The viscount felt his heart wrench, but none of his emotions showed in his face as he took her hand to help her down the few remaining steps.

The butler smiled indulgently at Maddie as he held the door, but directed his eyes rigidly forward as the viscount passed, his body stiff with disapproval.

"Oh, Charles," laughed Maddie, as he handed her into the carriage. "Did you see Thompson's face? I'm afraid you wounded him most deeply. You'll be lucky if he doesn't slam the door in your face next time!"

16

"I'll just stick my foot in the door," answered the viscount as he climbed into the carriage.

"And ruin the shine on your boot? That would be too bad, Charles."

"It would be worth it, love," he answered, signalling the horses to move forward. "Marry me, Maddie," he said after a few minutes.

Maddie laughed. "Charles, you are just too totally outrageous! Imagine proposing in the midst of all this traffic! How terribly flattering of you!"

"Would you say yes if I went down on my knees?"

"Definitely not in this mess!"

"Maddie, I'm serious."

"I know, Charles. We've been through this before. The answer is still no. Be my friend, not my lover."

"Yes, I know. But, my girl, if you knew the havoc you create when you smile so engagingly at me!"

"Come, Charles. Most of my attraction is because I'm always rebuffing you! If I married you, you would murder me within a sen'night!"

"Alas, it's quite true, my dear. Especially if you invited your most benevolent aunt to live with us!"

"Be kind, or we'll spend the rest of this drive in silence!"

"All right, but I'll never know why you invited the dragon to live with you."

"Charles, even a spinster of my advanced age cannot set up an establishment alone. The marchioness is the only relation I have that was free to come to live with me. Besides, I need her to keep away the riffraff!"

"Oh ho! Riffraff, am I? I'm wounded, Maddie. Seriously and deeply wounded!"

"As long as you don't perish before you negotiate that barouche, we'll be fine. Maybe I should take the reins while you recover from your swoon!"

17

The awkward moment was past, and the two spent the rest of the drive pleasurably baiting each other.

† † † † †

Maddie awoke late in the afternoon, for once grateful for the current vogue of napping in the afternoon. The double life was demanding, and it took a lot of juggling to keep it from totally exhausting her. Luckily the life of a woman of the *ton* was innately sedentary.

Maddie rolled over with a weary sigh. Yes, Marta was still there, and she wasn't intending to leave.

"Get up, Miss Maddie. It's time to get ready."

Maddie rolled stiffly out of bed and slipped into the dressing gown Marta was holding imperatively.

Marta expertly dressed Maddie's hair into a loose twist high on her head. The dark hair curled lovingly on Maddie's cheek and fell in soft curls to caress the smooth, white skin of her neck.

The rich, deep blue gown was gently dropped over the elegant coiffure, and the silver sash tied in place. Rich silver lacing graced the cuffs and hem, and sapphires in a silver setting glittered in her ears and hair. A heavy silver necklace set with sapphires and diamonds encircled the long, graceful neck and dropped deeply on the bosom discriminatingly exposed. Soft silver dancing shoes and a silver reticle completed the vision.

Maddie was pleasantly surprised as she critically observed her figure in the glass. The blue of the gown was reflected in her usually grey eyes, and the dark colour accented her height. Too thin, she thought, and turned away. Marta placed a silver mantle lined in deep blue on her shoulders as she moved to the door. A last adjustment to the long silver gloves was all that was needed before Maddie was ready to descend the stairs.

Maddie was gratified to see the approval in her aunt's face as she reached the foot of the stairs. A smile lifted at the corners of Maddie's lips. Aunt Agatha was a constant in her deep plum and gold. No one had, in all these years, dared remind the marchioness that purple and gold were reserved for royalty. One regal nod from her turbaned head was enough to quell any such impertinence. Cynics noted, however, that Lady Elverton's appearances in court were always attended in the same deep purple, but with silver accents. Only Aunt Agatha could sail so regally through the discrepancy.

Maddie turned her eyes to the slavishly adoring earl, who stood impatiently on the step. If only it were Charles instead of Edmund, thought Maddie with a sigh. Maybe then the evening wouldn't be a total waste.

Maddie moved through the ritual of greetings and allowed herself to be handed into the carriage. She stared unseeingly out the window and wished she was at that moment galloping recklessly across the heath.

The marchioness's ball proved to be an unmitigated success, and the announcement of their arrival was lost in the bustle.

"Quite a crush, Elizabeth," Lady Elverton greeted her hostess, and was soon whisked away for a coze with her cronies. Maddie allowed Edmund to find her a seat before he went off to procure a glass of champagne for her.

Maddie sat alone, exchanging greetings with acquaintances as they passed. After four years on the town, Maddie was well known in the limited circle of the *ton*. In a short time a small circle of friends and admirers had collected around her.

She was listening to the light banter of the group when Viscount Perry was announced. His quick scan of the room located Maddie immediately, and he made his way towards her with a casual nod to his acquaintances.

As he drew near, the Earl of Alvon appeared, carefully carrying two glasses of champagne. Maddie intercepted a devilish look from Charles and was torn between laughing and groaning.

"Let me help you, Lord Edmund," Charles offered, deftly removing a glass from the startled earl. "This, of course, must be for the lovely Miss Elverton. She informed me earlier that you had stolen the march on me! I was downcast," Charles ended with a dramatic sigh.

Lord Edmund hesitated, caught between a feeling of self-gratitude and a nagging suspicion that he was somehow being laughed at. In that brief pause, Charles triumphantly presented Maddie her glass with a deep bow.

Maddie's eyes were twinkling, but being aware of the earl's displeased frown, she accepted her drink demurely without further comment.

Charles then made the happy discovery of an acquaintance the earl must get to know. The unhappy lord was caught up in a conversation he could not politely remove himself from, and his pained expression caused Maddie to turn to Charles.

"I cannot be pleased with your actions, Lord Delvin."

"Yes, but you are, Maddie! You can't convince me that you were looking forward to a coze with that stuffy windbag! Be honest, Maddie!" he added, as Maddie opened her mouth to protest.

Maddie was too honest to deny it, so she snapped her mouth shut and turned a cold shoulder. Charles chuckled and sat idly listening to a heated debate that was developing within the group.

Maddie was grateful for a moment to let her mind wander. She was letting her eyes travel over the press of people, when her attention became riveted on a figure across the room. Surrounded by a large collection of young men, an entrancing woman could be glimpsed.

Maddie leaned over to Charles. "Who is that woman? I know I have never seen her before!"

"She was one of the Semple girls." Maddie's face puckered

with confusion. "Out a few years before you, love. Allie Semple made quite a splash with her come out, and in the end married a rake — broke his neck following the hounds, I believe. She was widowed a year ago, and I understand Lady Sifton has coaxed her back to London. Penniless, you know. Has to make a good match."

"Intriguing. I gather she's become the rage with the younger set?"

"An Incomparable, from what I understand. Better watch out, Maddie, or I'll lose my heart to another woman!"

"Oh, Charles, you are ridiculous. I *want* you to lose your heart to another woman!"

At that moment Charles's attention was recalled to the group by an insistent demand for his opinion, and Maddie was given the opportunity to try for a more satisfactory view of the latest Beauty. After so many years on the town she had seen many Diamonds of the First Water. As Maddie's was not a jealous nature, she enjoyed watching these Diamonds blaze across the season, only to see them married before the *ton* broke up to rusticate in the country.

Across the room the group of men shifted, and Maddie was able to see the Beauty clearly. She almost gasped at the sight. There, sitting proudly erect, was indeed a beauty. The rich, deep gold hair was pulled up severely, revealing beautifully carved cheekbones. Her head was perched regally on a long, slim neck, which was inclined slightly towards a handsome man in uniform. Her lips were parted slightly and her long, elegant fingers moved a delicate fan near her face.

Maddie watched in amazement at the graceful movement. Here was the language of the fan developed into a rare and beautiful art form. It coaxed, rebuffed, and refused as it flirted in her hand. Maddie became aware of how the fan had hypnotized her, and she glanced up to see who all this attention was being directed at. The Beauty was looking directly at her, and Maddie found herself sinking into the deep pools of the eyes of the woman across from her. The shifting, startling, deep, deep green of those eyes held her for long moments until, in horror, Maddie wrenched her eyes away.

Her breathing was heavy now, and she stared resolutely at her feet as she tried to regain her composure. All she knew was that something was intensely wrong, and that suddenly, all of reality had changed. Maybe she had been wrong. Surely she had read far too much into that single look. But Maddie could not bring herself to look again; could not bear to have the world shift so dizzyingly under her feet. Distantly she heard Lord Edmund reminding her of their dance and numbly allowed herself to be led out to the dance floor.

Feeling began to return as Lord Edmund's inane conversation slowly broke in on her attention. She answered absently and clung to his shoulder, causing Lord Edmund to believe that Maddie had finally decided to capitulate. Pressing her hand warmly, he attempted to communicate to his love that he understood her shyness.

Maddie was torn between dismay and laughter when she realized what was happening. What could she do with the earl now? If she refused him, he would feel that she had been playing fast and loose with him. She steeled herself for the scene that would undoubtedly result. She began to believe that the heat had momentarily overcome her, and that the whole situation had been the result of a tired, overheated mind.

Her eyes searched for the Vision in white and gold to prove to herself that she was simply imagining. Her clear eyes found the object of her search on the dance floor, in the arms of the officer who had been dancing attendance on the Beauty all evening. Standing, the Vision was not as tall as she had first appeared. She was delicately rounded, with swaying hips and dimpled arms. Suddenly, the movement of the waltz whirled the couple around, and Maddie saw the Vision's face over the officer's shoulder. There, looking directly into her eyes, the Beauty gave Maddie a very distinct look of desire.

Maddie was so startled that she missed a step, and only the earl's strong arms kept her from falling. Solicitously, he led her off the floor and, at her insistence that she was hot, propelled her through the long windows that led onto the balcony.

The cool air struck Maddie hard, and she stood grasping the low rail. Below, the sound of a fountain gurgled up to them and pinpoints of light glittered in the water.

"This is not real," thought Maddie, "I'm dreaming. Any moment I'll wake up, and find Marta scolding me."

Lord Edmund, strongly moved by the moonlight in Maddie's hair, pulled her into his arms and inexpertly planted a kiss on her mouth. Maddie's attention returned with a jerk; she struggled in his arms while he recited his proposal. Taking her resistance as shyness, he again tried to kiss her, this one falling decidedly askew. Maddie, in a rage, hauled back and slapped him hard across the face. It would have been more effective on a bull in rut; the slap only excited him further. Maddie was in a white heat now. All the confusion of that nightmare of an evening merged with her rage at Lord Edmund's assault, and Maddie laid her fist into the earl's jaw with all the anger and adrenaline in her wiry body.

No one but the earl could have been as shocked as Maddie, as she watched him stagger backward. The low rail caught him in the thigh and the bemused earl toppled over it, to land with a splash in the fountain below.

Maddie took one despairing look over the rail, but could only hear the enraged bellowing of the earl as he thrashed around in the fountain. Desperately, Maddie ran back into the ballroom to search for her aunt.

Lady Elverton was preparing to go down for supper when Maddie imperatively tugged on her sleeve. A few choice words caught the marchioness's full attention, and within minutes Lady Elverton had decorously withdrawn from the ballroom. She excused herself to her hostess, saying in low tones that Magdalena had been overcome by the heat, and quickly whisked Maddie out the door and into their carriage.

Two

Maddie was grateful for the silence of her aunt, but also dreaded the tirade that would occur when she arrived home. What could she say? How could she excuse herself? A pounding headache began to tear at her.

The silence continued as the carriage pulled up at their town house and the two ladies climbed the stairs. Inside, the footman removed their cloaks and withdrew. A resigned Maddie was making her way to the drawing room when her aunt's voice cut sharply.

"Go to bed, Magdalena."

Maddie turned questioningly to her aunt.

"We'll talk in the morning," her aunt continued, ominously. Maddie turned to the stairs.

25

"Maddie."

Maddie turned back to her aunt. Her aunt's face softened, and the marchioness lifted a gentle, wrinkled hand and touched Maddie's face. "Do you need draught for that headache, Maddie?"

Maddie stared blankly at her aunt for a moment.

"No, Aunt Agatha, I think I'll be all right. Thank you for caring."

"Go to bed now, Maddie," her aunt answered softly. Maddie opened her mouth to speak, but the old stern forbidding lines had returned to her aunt's face.

"Good night, Aunt," she muttered instead and slowly made her way upstairs.

† † † † †

Maddie winced as Marta pulled back the curtains the next morning. It had been an endless night of tossing and turning, and Maddie was no more ready to face the day than she had been last night. Still, she let Marta coax her out of bed, and she sat dejectedly at her dressing table.

Marta was silent. Word traveled fast among servants, and the Elverton household was buzzing with the news of last night's events. Quietly she helped Maddie dress, her face filled with sympathy and support.

At the door Maddie turned and gave Marta an impulsive hug before she descended the stairs.

Breakfast with Aunt Agatha ran rigidly on routine. The conversation dealt with Lady Elverton's plans for the day, and Maddie responded in low monosyllables, her mind shooting off in a million directions. She was frowning over her toast when her aunt rose from the table. The inevitable had come. With a heart more than ready to put all this mess behind her, she followed her aunt to the drawing room.

"Well, Magdalena," her aunt began as she seated herself,

"you're old enough to realize the consequence of your behavior last night. All of London will be buzzing with it. My Anne has informed me that the gossip has already managed to circulate to the servants here. It will be hard to rise above this. What are you planning to do?"

Maddie sank into a nearby chair. "I'm feeling very cowardly this morning, Aunt. Maybe I should retire until it all blows over."

"I was afraid of that, Maddie. Take the advice of an old campaigner. Send a message around for that disrespectful young viscount of yours, and get him to escort us to the theatre tonight."

"Aunt, please!"

"No, Magdalena, there's no backing down now. I will use my influence to help you through, but only *you* can take the wind out of their sails. You're a strong woman, Maddie. You'll survive the night."

"The only way?"

"The only way."

"Then I can withdraw with grace?"

"If the night is a success, then yes, you could take a breather for a few days, but not for very long. Let's avoid giving them more food for gossip. Now, go to bed, Magdalena. If you look peaked tonight everyone will know you didn't sleep a wink last night. I'll handle the morning callers for today."

In a burst of affection Maddie hugged her aunt, much to that lady's dismay.

"Really, Magdalena, you've quite crushed my dress!"

But the stern look could not hide the pleasure in Lady Elverton's eyes. Maddie smiled crookedly and went upstairs to wrestle with sleep.

† † † † †

When the viscount arrived, Maddie was looking forward to the evening. Tonight she would be outrageous and infinitely charming. The haughty matrons wouldn't know whether to disapprove or be captivated! She was dressed in grey with red stripes that bordered on the obscene. Even her hat echoed the impossible pattern. A riot of curls framed a face full of mischief and fun.

The viscount wondered whether anyone would notice the throbbing of his pulse, or the high flush in his cheeks, as he tried to avoid staring blankly at Maddie.

"Not your usual style, Maddie," he finally managed to say, grateful that his voice had not cracked. He continued lightly, "But it becomes you, my dear!"

"Do you like it, Charles?" Maddie asked, twirling around like a schoolgirl in her first party dress.

"Really, Magdalena! You go to far," cut in Lady Elverton severely. "We are attempting to *save* your reputation, not destroy it completely. If you can not behave properly, I'll have to remove my support completely. If you are ready, Lord Delvin, I believe we should be going."

Maddie and Charles exchanged looks full of amusement as they made their way out to the carriage. Charles's composure quickly returned, however, and he was rigidly formal as he handed Aunt Agatha into the coach.

As the coachman drove them quickly towards the theatre, Maddie turned her face to the window with a soft sigh. The afternoon had been long and sleepless as last night's events ran through her head, over and over again. In the end, she'd been forced to admit that she was undeniably attracted to another woman. Even now her mind shied from the ramifications of such a realization. How she wished this night were over. She needed a few days of quiet so she could pull together her disordered thoughts.

The theatre was crowded as the carriage pulled up. With a

mental shake, Maddie brought herself back to the task at hand. With a smile in place, she let Charles hand her down. The twinkle of humor returned to her eyes as they made their way to the viscount's box.

Lady Elverton took matters firmly in hand as soon as Lord Delvin had them comfortably situated. With imperious looks, she quelled any tendency of the young gentlemen below to stare at Magdalena, while with a regal nod she acknowledged the greetings of her acquaintances.

Magdalena watched her aunt admiringly through the corner of her eye as she engaged in light conversation with the viscount. As the curtain rose, Maddie realized that Charles would never be able to appreciate the inherent strength and style of Lady Elverton. He could never understand the nuances of what was being accomplished tonight by her determined and astute aunt.

The curtain came down on the first act much too soon for Maddie. Lady Elverton turned to the viscount. "I believe that Magdalena would like to stretch her legs, Lord Delvin," said Aunt Agatha, in a voice that brooked no refusal. "Magdalena, please bring me some refreshment. Hurry now, I see Elizabeth heading this way with her dreadful son."

Maddie escaped with Charles into the walkway behind their booth, and they began to stroll with the other fashionable couples there. Maddie greeted and chatted with friends as they made their way to the refreshment table.

Maddie was turning from the table with a lemonade for her aunt, when she saw Miss Alexandra Dinwiddie, on the arm of an ancient suitor, descending upon her with a look of malicious pleasure on her face. Maddie knew with a sinking heart that there was no escaping the encounter.

"Hello, Magdalena," said Miss Dinwiddie. The thin smile on her lips failed to hide the antagonism in her eyes. "I see you managed to get an escort tonight."

"Hello, Alexandra. It's good to see you, too," said Maddie, deliberately ignoring the insult in Alexandra's tone. "Are you enjoying the performance?"

Alexandra was frustrated by the balking of her prey. Undaunted, she continued, "Oh, not nearly as much as the goings on in the seats. I noticed that you draw a great deal of attention to yourself. You should be careful of your reputation, Magdalena. Certainly you have enough trouble without flouncing around on the arm of a notorious rake."

Magdalena felt the anger coursing through her system. For a moment she considered dashing the lemonade into that smug face. Instead, she smiled with a sickening sweetness. "I didn't even notice, Alexandra. How nice of you to keep track of the slights directed at me by individuals far outside the *haut ton*. Indeed, I would not even know their names, but I'm sure you will be able to inform me."

For a moment she thought Alexandra would try to slap her, but Miss Dinwiddie was too much in control to create such a scene. Still, Maddie would have sworn that she heard that very proper young woman grind her teeth in a very unladylike manner.

Miss Dinwiddie opened her mouth for an ill-advised retort, when Lord Delvin came up to take Maddie back to the booth. Gratefully, Maddie turned from her antagonist. Placing a hand on the viscount's arm, she looked up and saw the Vision from last night staring at her. The beautiful Allie Sifton nodded her admiring approval before she passed by on the arm of her officer suitor. Maddie's heart swelled in response, and she felt like dancing back to the booth. It was amazing to her, the effect of that simple look, and yet somehow the whole evening was brighter because of it.

30

Maddie yawned and stretched luxuriously as the morning sun spilled into her room. Happy dreams of the past night had accompanied her sleep, and she smiled as she lounged in bed. She was enjoying the delicious moments of quiet solitude. She delayed ringing for breakfast as she lay listening to the sounds of the day.

Aunt Agatha had termed the evening a rout, and Maddie had smiled in agreeance. Allie Sifton's presence had been the sweetening of the pot. Even now, the memory of that look could cause erraticacies in her system, causing her head to feel quite light, and Maddie knew that she had to have more of that tantalizing presence.

She lay plotting impossible "accidental" meetings, but never could decide what to do after enacting a rendezvous. The direct "Hello, I'm Maddie, and I'm madly in love with you!" would surely get her locked up! What if she had fatally misinterpreted the Beauty's looks? No, surely that was impossible. That first look had been so caressing and gentle. Certainly she could not have misread such a message!

On the other hand, a simple meeting in, say, the Circulating Library would hardly lend itself to serious discussion, and even if they were alone, would Allie make the first move?

Her thoughts ran in long, circuitous patterns, much to her despair. The only answer was to start the day and put such stewings behind her for awhile. With great decision she rang for Marta to bring her breakfast.

Marta bustled in almost immediately and informed Maddie that her tray would be up shortly. She then proceeded to fluff Maddie's pillows, to that young woman's distress.

"Marta," Maddie started, attempting to distract the industrious maid. "Marta, I'm going out tonight."

Marta's hands paused for a brief moment, then continued as she heaved a meaning-laden sigh. After so many years with

Maddie, Marta knew the futility of argument. She simply nodded and directed the placement of Maddie's breakfast tray
brought up by a chambermaid.

Three

Maddie gave a final tug to her black gloves and eased her horse forward to the edge of the glade. She breathed deeply, enjoying air free from the smells of the city. Above, the stars glittered in a magnificent blanket that reached down to caress the horizon. A benevolent moon shone serenely, almost smiling at her, and Maddie felt the power of the night flowing through her as she listened to the sounds of the evening. She sat her horse and reveled in the feeling of being home.

The mood was not to last, however. From the distance came the sound of a ponderous coach slowly tooling towards her. An eager smile flashed on her face as she gathered herself for action. She felt she would explode with excitement as she waited on the agonizing pace of the coach. With any luck the slow speed indicated wealth-laden travelers on their way to London.

At last the coach was drawing abreast, and Maddie's horse exploded under her as she pressed her heels to his sides. Catching sight of unanticipated motion from the corner of her eye, she desperately tried to check his flight, wrenching him to the left with a tug that brought his head up as a shower of bullets flew around her. In almost crazed fear, she slammed her heels into her horse and together they shot away into the glade.

Unchecked, she directed the surging gelding towards the narrow path that led deeper into the woods. Behind her the sound of pursuit echoed in the silence. She flattened herself along her horse's neck to avoid being swept off by the low branches. Grateful to the moon for her unfaltering light and the steadiness of her mount, she flew on through the night.

The sounds of pursuit were fainter now, and the initial paralyzing throes of fear had begun to ease. She knew that any determined pursuer would only have to follow the path through the woods. The meadow where the trail would lead would give them a clear shot at her dark back in the full light of the moon.

In a moment of decision, she stopped her horse and turned him into the thick growth at the edge of the path. Slowly, they began to wind their way through the trees. It was frustrating work, as time and time again they had to turn back after reaching an impassable clump of growth.

Her gelding heard the horses passing on the path before Maddie was aware of their closeness. She stopped him as soon as she noticed the flick of his ears. With a fervent prayer, she willed him to remain silent until the pursuers were out of hearing range. She uttered a sigh of relief and gave him a grateful pat of thanks before easing him forward.

It would only be a matter of minutes before they discovered

that she was not in front of them. Would there be enough of them to block the roads around the woods? How quickly could they organize? How could she have walked into such a simple trap? She closed her eyes for a moment and relived the horror of seeing the guard of soldiers coming up behind the coach. Only their distance behind the coach, probably to avoid any telltale noise, had saved her. Her heart was sinking in despair. Could she outwit an organized trap?

To her relief, Maddie reached the edge of the woods before panic could take its grip on her. She halted on the fringe of the trees, listening and watching. In a moment of decision, she launched her horse forward and tore across the field at a break-neck pace, hoping her sure-footed steed would not fall into a disastrous hole. She felt a surge of relief as no sounds of pursuit reached her ears. She veered off, aiming for a nearby road.

She almost laughed aloud as she listened to the sound of her horse's hooves drumming along the hard-packed dirt of the road. She'd done it! She'd made it! She slowed her horse to a canter now, breezing him past a small hamlet.

A small scream escaped her lips as a huge charger burst from behind a cottage. She leveled her horse out along the road with the soldier in hot pursuit. Her gelding stretched full out in a noble attempt to give her more, but was no match for the fresh speed of the soldier's mount, who quickly pulled alongside.

As they raced level, the soldier threw himself across her, bearing her to the ground with the force of his weight. In a lucky twist, Maddie managed to land on top of the soldier, who took the brunt of the fall. Desperately, she tried to wrench away as he fought to catch his wind, but she couldn't manage to break his meaty grip. She clawed his face, but her gloves made her nails ineffective weapons.

Almost instinctively, she sank her teeth deep into his forearm, causing him to break his grip. She rolled away and

35

dragged her pistol from her cloak. Having no time to cock it, she slammed the handle against his head as he launched himself at at her. In panic, she hit him again before she realized he was still.

She rolled him over and grimaced at the huge slash down his cheek. She wasted little concern, however, when she saw a gentle rising of his chest. Checking under his great cloak for a weapon, she got a closer look at his face.

"Good Lord," she thought, "Allie's officer!" and, for a moment she almost let the horror of the nightmare wash over her. Drawing on the deep inner strength that had brought her this far, she turned to look for her horse.

Her gelding had continued his flight, but the officer's mount had obviously stopped immediately upon the loss of weight as the rider left the saddle. Moving slowly, she approached him. He stood patiently as she gathered up the reins and mounted him. Obediently, he moved out on her cue, and she started down the road to find her horse.

She found him standing beside the road, his head down to his knees, his lathered sides heaving. With a caressing word, she leaned over to grasp his reins and began to lead him slowly to the outskirts of London. There she dismounted the officer's horse and sent him off into the night with a slap. She mounted her own gelding and began to make her way slowly home.

† † † † †

Marta whisked her upstairs without a word, as Maddie came in the door. The prelight of dawn meant the house would soon be astir with servants. With amazing efficiency, Marta undressed Maddie and hid away her clothes. Still in silence, she washed the grime and dirt smears from Maddie's face. In minutes, Maddie was abed and Marta gone. Maddie grimaced to herself. Marta's rigid silence meant a lecture was in order as soon as Marta was sure everything was safe.

With a groan she lay back against the pillows and tried to relax a body filled with jangling nerves. Her stomach was in a tight knot of anxiety. What a fiasco the night had been! What would happen now? What if no one found Allie's officer, and he died?

The host of worries chased around her head and she lay in wide-eyed despair. She jumped as Marta entered, bearing a steaming cup.

"Drink this, Moppet," said Marta soothingly. "Everything will be fine. Everything has been taken care of."

Marta stroked Maddie's head soothingly as she sipped her drink. When Maddie finished she handed Marta her cup with a self-conscious glance, but Marta hushed her before she could speak. She slipped down under the covers and looked drowsily at Marta, who continued to stroke her hair. In a minute Marta's brew had taken hold, and she slipped off into a deep sleep.

† † † † †

The sun was bright in the sky when Maddie awoke. Surely last night had just been a bizarre dream. She lay in bed and let the sun soak into her.

Marta came in, announcing that Lady Elverton would like to know whether Maddie was going to sleep all day.

"I'm getting up, Marta. I want to wear my dark green walking dress. Could you arrange to have my phaeton ready after I'm through talking with the marchioness?"

"First you'll have your tea and toast. You're looking a little pulled around the eyes. How much trouble did you get into last night?"

"I don't know, Marta. We'll have to wait and see. At least my identity wasn't revealed. Keep your ears cocked for any news. Anything at all unusual."

"Maybe now you'll stop this nonsense?"

"I can't. You know that. Our road is fixed, Marta, and I

37

wouldn't have it any other way. But if an acceptable way out is offered, you know I'd jump on it in a flash. I'm tired of being shot at," Maddie added with a crooked grin.

Marta snorted and turned to the wardrobe to find the requested walking dress.

† † † † †

Maddie's features were set in a frown as she made her way down to the stables. Aunt Agatha had expressed concern over Maddie's seeming inability to recover from all the late night gaiety. To Maddie's dismay, the marchioness was considering an early withdrawal from London. Although Maddie had been hasty to reassure her aunt, she was not sure whether her protestations had swayed the marchioness from her intended course. An early departure to the country would mean disaster for Maddie's plans.

Maddie was so intent in following her thoughts that it was a moment before she was aware of the cool cobblestones under her feet and the warm, friendly smell of the horses. Heads popped over the half-doors at the sound of her arrival, and here and there an old acquaintance would nicker a greeting.

As always, the gentle acceptance of the horses drew her out of herself and away from her own problems as she moved down the aisle, stopping a moment to talk to each one.

Her intention was to see how her gelding had recovered from the night before. She was approaching his stall when a young groom popped out of one of the stalls. Maddie smiled at his startled expression as he realized her presence. For a moment, Maddie thought he might dash away. Instead, he doffed his cap and bobbed in greeting.

"Good day, Miss Elverton. Henry has the phaeton ready at the front door."

"Yes, I know. I've come to see Fabian. How is he?"

"I don't rightly know, Miss Maddie. I worry about him, although Henry says I shouldn't fuss. Doesn't make sense to me, though, how a horse used so little can be so tired. But he appears to be fine, else. So maybe Henry's right."

Maddie nodded. Her demure smile hid the laughter in her eyes. She brushed past the groom and went into the gelding's stall.

Hello, Fabian," she greeted him. He rested his head on her shoulder and they stood in quiet communion for several minutes. They exchanged deep sighs before Maddie gave him a final pat. She walked slowly up the path towards the front of the house, her mind still back in the quiet coolness of the stable.

Henry was walking the flighty young horse that Maddie often drove to the park. He noticed her distant expression and refrained from making any comments about keeping young horses standing. He handed her up in silence and nimbly climbed up on his perch.

Maddie collected the reins and gave the horse office to start. She made her way to the park with only half a mind on the traffic and was surprised when she realized they had reached the entrance. With a conscious effort she settled an appropriate smile on her uncurved lips. To distract herself, she began to scan the drive for her acquaintances.

Almost immediately she spotted Charles near a handsome landau. Closer inspection revealed Allie Sifton sitting with an elderly woman, who had a magnificent coiffure of white hair. They were stopped along the path, so there was no way to avoid a meeting without giving offense.

Maddie urged her horse along, hoping to be able to pass with a simple nod of greeting. She was almost level when Charles waved her over. For a brief moment Maddie wondered if a heart could soar and fall at the same moment. Before she could decide, she was alongside the landau, and Charles was introducing her.

39

"Lady Sifton, Countess, this is Miss Elverton. Magdalena, this is Lady Sifton, Marchioness of Quiton, and Allie Sifton, Countess of Fawnhope."

Maddie uttered an appropriate reply as she brushed hands with Lady Sifton. Allie lifted her hand with an engaging smile, and Maddie felt the power of Allie's touch surging through her as she looked deeply into the shifting green of Allie's eyes. Embarrassed, she wrenched her gaze away before the rest of the party noticed the exchange.

"It's very daring of you to be driving your own carriage, Miss Elverton," Lady Sifton said, admiringly. "I was remarking to Lord Delvin how bold young people are these days. I'm afraid that I would shock my associates if I admitted that I'm envious of the freedom you young ladies enjoy."

Maddie turned her attention to the remarkable Lady Sifton. In an era when pale, unmarked skin was the vogue, Lady Sifton's face would always cause a stir. The marchioness's countenance was a nut brown, with deep smile lines and crow's feet at the corners of snapping brown eyes. It was a face full of laughter, even when she was not smiling, and it glowed with an inner light. Maddie's own lips curved up in response to that laughter, and she wondered why such a joyous face would somehow remind her of Aunt Agatha.

"Some consider me a little too bold, Lady Sifton. However, if you would allow me to teach you to drive, I'm sure it would become quite the rage!" Maddie answered lightly.

"I'm much too old to be overturned trying to keep up with you, my dear. I do, however, like the style of the whole thing. Maybe I could talk you into taking my niece on as your pupil. She's too young to spend her life behind a coachman." The marchioness threw a derisive glance at the stiffened back of her own coachman.

"Maybe you could take her for a ride around the park,

while I have this handsome young man to act as an escort." She gave Charles a bold wink that almost made Maddie sputter with laughter. Charles rose nobly to the occasion, bowing low over his horse, with a roguish twinkle in his eye.

Maddie's groom hopped down from his perch to hand the countess up into the phaeton. After Allie was securely settled, he moved to regain his position, but was stopped by Maddie.

"Wait for me here, Henry, I'll be fine without you." She gave her horse office to start.

"The viscount called you Magdalena. May I also?" enquired Allie after a few minutes.

"Actually, everyone calls me Maddie. I feel more comfortable with that. I understand you are Allie. Shall I call you that?"

"Please. You've heard my name, then. Have you been interested in me?"

Maddie kept her mouth firmly shut in order to keep her jaw from dropping. Was it the simple question it seemed, or did it have deeper undertones? She willed herself to concentrate. Somehow she had to avoid falling into those unsure currents.

"I suppose that any new face must draw interest from those who have been on the town for so many seasons."

"As you have. I have been wondering why you have not married. Certainly, you would be quite a catch for some lucky fellow."

"I'm afraid that most men are looking for a woman with more than an independence. Surely you know how important it is to have wealth in the circles of the *ton?*"

"And yet, there are men to whom this wouldn't matter. Wealthy, well-bred gentlemen would gladly offer for you. Lord Delvin, for example."

"I guess I'm too picky. I would not be very happy as a viscountess."

"You would be a spinster, than marry without love? You

must be a very strong-minded woman. I was not that strong."

"My aunt considers me stubborn. You are sensible."

"Not always so sensible," Allie said softly, almost under her breath. Maddie knew it was not a statement to answer. Silence lay peacefully between them for a moment, until Allie leaned over and brushed her fingers across Maddie's gloved hand that held lightly to the reins.

"You have very strong hands. You must ride a great deal," she said.

Maddie was startled for a moment. "Not too often when I'm in town," she answered, hoping Allie would not concentrate too much on that detail.

"My hands always lose their tone when I don't ride. Yours seem so hard."

Maddie felt like groaning aloud. "Maybe it's because I drive myself to the park so often," Maddie said desperately. "When you begin to drive I'm sure you'll notice a difference in your own hands."

Allie seemed satisfied with her answer, and Maddie almost sighed with relief. She would have to be careful around Allie. A careless word repeated to her officer escort could destroy Maddie's world. Thinking of the officer drove Maddie to speak again.

"I've become used to seeing you with an officer. Did he lose the privilege of escorting you to the park?"

"Lt. Bridgewater? He's an old friend of my late husband. I'm not acquainted with many people in town yet, and he's been kind enough to accompany my aunt and me on a few excursions. I'm afraid he's been laid up for a few days. He sent me a hasty note cancelling our ride today, but he didn't give a reason. It may have something to do with his assignment here, so he wouldn't be able to say anything."

"Assignment? Here? What is it? A murder?"

42

"Actually, he's tracking a highway robber. Isn't it exciting? I guess there is an intrepid bandit who is terrorizing the roads in and out of London. He must be very smart, because they haven't been able to catch him. The lieutenant says he seems to have an instinct for avoiding traps, and he uses an erratic pattern that makes him hard to outguess. I wonder how desperate he is? Do you think he could be dangerous?"

Maddie almost blinked. If they were referring to her, she had certainly been luckier than she had realized. Instinct? Certainly not! Luck had been her guide!

"I don't know. I haven't heard of such a robber," Maddie said innocently. "Has he killed anyone?"

"Michael didn't say. I don't think so. I think he just blusters them. Still, one never knows!"

"Well, I hope the lieutenant is successful in his search. It's enough to make one stay in London!"

"Not my aunt! She thinks it would be terribly exciting to be held up! She tells me it would do wonders to break up the monotony. Besides, she'd be able to tell everyone about it in excruciating detail!"

Maddie was grateful that they had reached the landau once more, and she was spared the anguish of trying to answer. She watched Allie alight with a sad look. She had only begun to scratch the surface of that intriguing personality. She had managed, however, to gain a glimpse of a mind that was sharp and alert. Maddie looked forward to an opportunity to touch that mind once more.

The two parties exchanged invitations for a day visit and parted on complacent terms. Maddie decided to return home. If Allie didn't have news of the lieutenant, then no one would. The note indicated he was alive and conscious. She was concerned that he would soon be turning all his attention back to catching her. She would go out again tonight, before he was up and about. She hoped they would have slackened their guard, believing her to be scared off. If she had a big take tonight, she could lay low for awhile, and maybe the excitement would blow over.

† † † † †

Maddie reined in her tired horse and sat quietly along the roadside. Tonight had been a night of daring insanity. Already she had held up two carriages along the same road as the night before. Lady Luck had been smiling broadly on her this evening, and she had started home with a heavy, jingling purse. She had decided to ride into London along a different road and had exhausted her gelding, pushing him hard across country. Now, after gaining the road, she heard a carriage coming up behind her. A little spirit of devilry made her decide to hold up this coach, too.

In the pattern long familiar to both her and her horse, she stopped the coach with a single shot. Quickly, she rode over and wrenched the carriage door open, and demanded in a gruff voice that the passengers step down.

She watched in horror as Lady Sifton and Allie stepped out into the light of the carriage lanterns. It was much too late to back out now. With a sudden decision, she dismounted her horse and approached the ladies.

"Quick now! Let's see those jewels. Come on, come on! Hand it over!" She held out her hand demandingly to Lady Sifton. The pistol in her hand moved threateningly. When the fear wore off, Maddie hoped that the marchioness would be delighted with the whole encounter. Still, it was hard to watch that crinkled face devoid of its entrancing smile.

Maddie turned to Allie and lifted the diamonds from her shaking hand. It wrenched her deep inside to see that strained, pale face. Those deep green eyes were dark with terror now.

"It's all right, my lady," Maddie murmured softly. She

44

stripped off her glove and gently caressed Allie's face. "I would never consider hurting such a beautiful woman." Unable to control the urge, she ran a loving hand through Allie's thick gold hair. "So precious," she murmured.

Allie's studying look brought Maddie back to herself. Gruffly now, she demanded Lady Sifton's purse. Shoving the loot in her pockets, she turned crisply away and swiftly mounted her gelding. Without a word she dashed away down the road. She was disconcerted when a backward look caught Allie staring hard after her.

Four

It was almost a week later when Maddie finally saw Allie again. She was sitting in the front room with Lady Elverton when Lady Sifton and Allie were announced. Maddie was surprised to see Aunt Agatha falter in her stitching before directing Thompson to show them up. It was the first time Maddie had seen the marchioness appear even slightly disconcerted.

Lady Sifton paused in the doorway, her eyes on Aunt Agatha's pale face.

"Agatha," she said softly, entering with her hands stretched forward.

Lady Elverton rose and clasped Lady Sifton's hands. With a little choke in her voice, she murmured, "Constance, it's been an age!"

The two women stared into each other's eyes for a moment before returning to the present.

Lady Sifton recovered first. "Agatha, this is my niece, Allie Sifton," she said, encouraging Allie to come up from behind her.

"I believe you've already met Magdalena," said Lady Elverton, her composure completely restored.

"Yes, we had a nice coze in the park the day we were held up."

"London has been thick with rumors. I'm afraid it's going to be a Seven Day Wonder!"

The ladies settled as Lady Sifton told a lively tale of the robbery. Maddie hardly recognized herself as the huge, ferocious villain, and was highly entertained by the marchioness's embellishments. She was relieved that Lady Sifton made no mention of her attention to Allie. Undoubtedly, the marchioness had edited that part to preserve Allie's reputation.

The two marchionesses soon had their heads together discussing mutual acquaintances, and Maddie and Allie were able to continue discussing the notorious villain without interruption.

"Has Lt. Bridgewater been able to find any clues on the identity of the highwayman?" enquired Maddie.

"Actually, he has a very unusual theory," Allie said, staring hard at Maddie. "He believes the robber to be a woman."

Maddie managed to avoid jumping or flashing a guilty look at Allie, but there was no way she could stop the blood she felt rising to her cheeks. "Why would he suspect something like that? Surely that would be impossible?"

"He managed to wrestle the highwayman down one night. He remembers being surprised at the thief's slight build, and then he was knocked unconscious. He's convinced that the robber is either a boy or a woman."

"You have met the infamous highwayman, now. Do you agree with the lieutenant?" Maddie kept her eyes focused on her feet to hide the intensity of her question. A moment of silence

47

passed and Maddie was forced to look up into the direct gaze focused on her. Allie's thoughts were unfathomable.

Maddie was torn between the agony of waiting and the pleasure of having Allie's full attention on her. Even as she held her breath, she knew she could get lost so easily in those eyes.

After a moment Allie drew a long breath of decision and answered, "No, I think the highwayman must be a man." She opened her mouth to say more, but snapped it firmly shut.

Maddie was intensely curious as to what Allie would have continued to say, but knew from Allie's expression that she would get no response. A perverse part of her was crushed by Allie's answer, even though it was what she wanted to hear. Maddie gave herself a mental shake. There would have only been trouble if Allie had agreed with the lieutenant. It seemed her heart was determined to lead her into trouble lately.

With determination Maddie picked up the threads of the conversation and continued. "Then the highwayman must be in a desperate situation, certainly? Wouldn't the lieutenant have pity on a young man driven to steal?"

"Oh no! When the lieutenant was knocked out, the thief's cruel blow split his cheek. It's going to leave a nasty scar, which is something he'll never forgive. I'm afraid Michael had a high opinion of his looks. Now I can't even convince him to go out in public, and until it heals properly, I can't really blame him."

"Is he retiring from the search, then, until he is more presentable?"

"No. In fact, I think the scar has made him slightly crazy. He's out all night searching, setting up traps, and trying to out-trick the villain. His inability to find any trace of the bandit just makes him more frenzied. Sometimes I'm afraid to be around him with all that untapped anger waiting to flare out. I think he could be very violent."

"Then it's just as well he's not going out in society. I would hate to think of you alone with him. Your safety is too important to risk with an unstable escort."

Allie cocked her head at Maddie, and Maddie quickly dropped her eyes. It was with great relief that Maddie heard Allie continue.

"Speaking of escorts, Maddie, are you going to Lady Anne's masquerade ball?"

"My aunt doesn't approve of masquerades, so I'm sure she wouldn't allow me to attend. Are you going to go?"

"Oh, yes! Of course! Lady Sifton would never consider missing anything so dashing. In fact, she's going in costume. I believe as a page boy! Isn't she daring? I can't wait to be a lively dowager! Think of the freedom she has! If anyone fusty peers down their nose at her she just snaps her fingers at them! She's too rich to be ignored, so they call her "eccentric," and make her welcome in all circles of the *ton*. I'm too envious for words."

"But at least you get to go! Are you going in costume, too?"

"I'm afraid I'm too demure, but I have a beautiful silver domino to wear. I hope I'll be the only one in the room, but you know what a crush it will be. Still it's better than pink or black. Have you noticed how everyone chooses those colors?"

Maddie nodded as Lady Sifton cut in, "Allie, my dear, we are free tomorrow afternoon, aren't we? Lady Agatha and I have decided on an excursion. A day in the country would do us all a world of good."

"There's just your fitting for your masquerade costume."

"Ah, bah! Well, I'll just have to bully Suzette into coming early! She will not be able to resist my charm!"

Allie snorted, but said nothing as Lady Constance focused her challenging and yet playful glance on her.

"It's settled then," Lady Constance announced. "Maddie, we shall leave it to you to invite our escorts. You young people should be free to ride, while Lady Agatha and I sit in our fusty curricle." Lady Constance's laugh filled the room, and Maddie knew this little woman was capable of keeping up with the youngest of them despite her words.

"Allie, we really must go if we are to reach the Library before all of London! I shall be here promptly tomorrow, Lady Agatha, to pick you up. Until then!"

Lady Constance breezed out with Allie in tow, leaving the room still vibrating with her energy. Maddie was surprised to see her aunt's smile, but said nothing.

Both women felt reluctant to break the silence, and in peaceful accord they settled back and resumed their stitchery. Maddie waited until her aunt was engrossed in her work before secretively opening her handkerchief on the sofa next to her. Her slender fingers gently caressed the glittering diamond earring lying there, before she tucked it away. As she bowed her head over her embroidery a loving, almost impish smile rested on her lips.

† † † † †

The morning of the planned expedition dawned clear and cool, and Maddie was a bundle of nerves. Even Aunt Agatha seemed to be affected by the excitement of the morning. The breakfast ritual was rigidly adhered to, however, and Maddie could only be relieved when she was able to slip upstairs and change into her riding habit.

She was smiling as Marta slipped the maroon habit over her head. How she had argued with Lady Elverton when she had made the purchase! Aunt Agatha could not feel that red was an appropriate color for a single lady, but Maddie loved the rich material and the military look of the black lacing. She knew the color could only be flattering to her dark good looks.

She almost clapped her black-gloved hands in delight as she stood before her mirror. She had admitted to herself that she wanted to attract Allie's attention today, and she had agonized over every detail to get the desired effect.

She was fussing with her hat when the sound of the carriage wheels on the gravel below sent Maddie bounding to the window. There was Allie, in soft shades of green, on a dainty chestnut mare. Lady Constance, with her parasol tilted too far back to protect the already nut brown face, had also arrived.

Maddie was about to pull back to avoid being caught like a schoolgirl peering from the window, when Lord Edmund and Charles rode into the yard. Maddie gave a heavy sigh. She had no idea what Lady Elverton had done to convince the earl to attend the outing, but from the sour look on his face she knew that the heavy guns had been brought in.

She sank into her chair for a moment. She felt she could have handled the earl, but Lord Delvin's face had a devilish gleam that did not augur well for the day ahead. With brisk decision, she rose and moved determinedly to join her aunt in the hall.

The two women exchanged encouraging nods with each other before they exited to face their guests. Greetings were exchanged and, as Lady Sifton was in a hurry to start, no time was spent on trivialities.

Lord Edmund turned a cold shoulder to Maddie and solicitously handed Lady Elverton into the curricle. His marked attention to her aunt caused Maddie to smile derisively, and she allowed Charles to hand her up onto her mare.

"Please be good, Charles!" Maddie pleaded in an undertone.

"Never fear, dearest, I shall not let that old Friday face ruin the day," Charles answered with an impish twinkle.

"Just don't provoke him!"

"It'll be hard not to, Maddie!"

Maddie opened her mouth to answer, but the viscount was gone. At last everyone was ready, and the cavalcade began to make its way out of London.

The gentlemen of the party rode on either side of the open

carriage as an escort. Maddie and Allie followed behind, riding close to each other. The two spent the time talking comfortably about little odds and ends, and Maddie found herself able to relax and truly be herself.

She had a flash of resentment as they reached the quiet road outside London. Charles and Lord Edmund were waiting for her and Allie to catch up to them, and Maddie was more than reluctant to have those two break into her comfortable coze with Allie.

"Let's just race past them," Allie said in low tones.

Maddie turned to Allie's merry face and, after a moment's hesitation, nodded. Allie touched her heels into her horse, who responded instantly. Maddie's delayed reaction cost her ground, but soon she was flying along in hot pursuit.

They passed Lord Edmund and the viscount with hardly a glance and continued to tear down the deserted road. Maddie felt her mare stretch out and knew that her long strides would soon outdistance Allie's smaller mare.

Allie drew up her horse as Maddie came alongside. Both women dissolved into tears of laughter as they came to a stop. The race had been exhilarating, and the two exchanged a special, soft look of kinship. Maddie was about to reach out to touch Allie's arm when Lord Edmund and Charles arrived.

"Countess, Miss Elverton, are you all right? I suspected that that big mare was too much for you to handle, Magdalena. I have no doubt that reckless animal caused the countess's horse to bolt."

Maddie felt a surge of anger and exasperation at the earl's words. "No, Lord Edmund, we just indulged in a little race."

Maddie felt a glimmer of pleasure at the earl's startled and disapproving expression.

"It was great fun!" Allie added, convincing the affronted lord that the two were devoid of all sensibility. Maddie felt vindicated to see him at a loss for words.

By this time they had been joined by the ladies in the carriage, and Lady Agatha immediately began what was intended to be a lengthy dissertation on Maddie's reckless and unladylike behavior.

She had barely gotten "Magdalena, really!" out, before Lady Sifton cut in merrily.

"Yes, the two of you! Riding *ventra a terra* while your poor aunts are stuck in this stodgy carriage. I'm sure I don't know how to handle the envy it arouses. Please don't do it again! You can see that even Lord Edmund is sour about missing the fun!"

Both Lady Elverton and the earl were silenced by Lady Constance's words, and neither appeared pleased. However, in politeness to the marchioness, nothing more was said. Maddie and Allie shot Lady Constance a grateful look before proceeding at a more decorous pace alongside the carriage.

Lord Delvin, determined to make the party a success, flirted outrageously with Lady Sifton, and their light banter smoothed over the uncomfortable minutes.

The party reached its destination in good time. It was Lady Sifton's plan that the younger members of the group should spend their time exploring the old abbey, while Lady Agatha and herself had a comfortable coze in the shade. They would all meet back near the carriage for a picnic lunch before making their way back to London.

Lord Edmund and Allie fell into step behind Lord Delvin and Maddie. They proceeded at a leisurely pace, and the two lords discovered a mutual passion for crypts. Their conversation quickly moved on to war, and Allie and Maddie found themselves forgotten by their two escorts.

With a look of agreement, they left the men arguing hotly about whether the duel should have been outlawed, and made their way back into the sunshine. They strolled down to the little stone pond and stood quietly watching the swans.

"Aren't men silly?" Allie broke into the silence.

53

"Like little boys," agreed Maddie.

Allie sighed. "I find it very difficult to think of marrying one again. I would very much rather live on my own, but Aunt Constance says it just can't be done. If I had money I would never marry again!"

"Allie Sifton, I can see you're destined to become eccentric!"

"It wouldn't be so bad! You shouldn't laugh! If I lived in the country, what would I care if people thought I was eccentric?"

"Better than being on the shelf, I suppose."

"Maybe we should set up house together, and you can be my old maid companion!"

Maddie laughed and shook her head. She plopped herself down on a dilapidated bench. In her heart she knew that that was all she could desire. She also was intensely aware that this was just idle thinking on Allie's part and that she'd best keep her emotion to herself.

"Oh, Allie. You must realize that our aunts would be quite stubbornly disapproving! Lady Agatha has her heart set on me marrying into some prestigious family who can trace their ancestry back to William the Conqueror. It would be too bad of me if I just bowed out now!" Maddie's voice was light but she felt a heaviness in her chest. She felt that at any moment her voice would break into a sob.

Allie's face was pinched into a pout, and Maddie felt strong feelings of love as Allie flounced down on the bench next to her. Allie sat with her fine face resting on her two dainty fists. She looked more like a child from the nursery than the sophisticated lady Maddie had been so much in awe of.

"You're sulking!" Maddie accused.

"Well, why not! It's a great plan. I don't know why you have to be so stubborn. Surely you like me?"

"Of course I do," answered Maddie, trying to keep the intensity out of her voice. "However, I simply cannot see you in rags, feeding chickens. It's too preposterous!"

"I suppose you're right," said Allie in a voice full of doubt. "I'll just have to think of another way, and then I will insist on you being my companion."

"Until then," said Maddie, trying to keep up her end of the game. Could the ache in her chest get any larger?

Charles and Lord Edmund came up, having discovered the desertion of the two young ladies. To make up for their former distractions they now lavished elaborate attention on the ladies until Maddie found herself ready to vent her feelings on the group. Luckily, for the harmony of the party, it was time to join the older ladies and for Maddie it came none too soon.

They quietly approached their sleeping chaperones and Maddie lost her bad temper in the comic picture before her. Lady Agatha was sleeping upright against the trunk of a tree. Even in sleep she was controlled, but her mouth betrayed her. It was slightly open and emanating the sounds of deep sleep. Lady Constance, on the other hand, was as carefree in sleep as she was in life. Her head had dropped onto Lady Elverton's shoulder, pushing her hat to a decidedly askew position. To Maddie she looked like a schoolgirl who had fallen asleep against the banister while watching a ball she was too young to attend. It was an image that lingered, even as the two ladies awoke.

Lady Elverton was the first to awaken, her jaw snapping shut with a sharp click. The sound startled Lady Sifton, who scrambled upright, her eyes wide, and then relaxing as she became oriented.

"Well, Agatha, it looks like we overslept. Maybe we could cajole these young people into keeping our appearance to themselves!" Lady Constance said. She had recovered first and was unconcernedly rearranging her hat.

Lady Elverton rose immediately and moved to the carriage to direct the placement of the luncheon feast.

"I'm sure they are aware of decorum," was all Lady Agatha would say in answer to Lady Constance.

Maddie shot a repressing glance to Charles, to which he responded with a falsely innocent shrug. Lord Edmund was quick to reassure the ladies, and Maddie was sure she detected a gleam of humor in Lady Agatha's eyes as she brusquely cut across the lord's impassioned speech.

Lord Edmund found himself at a loss as the rest of the party responded to Lady Agatha's announcement that the meal was ready. His passionate nature was deeply injured by the callous response to his poetic speech, but, as no one seemed aware of his sulking, he soon became bored with it and joined into the conversation.

Maddie found no further chance to talk privately with Allie. Lord Delvin chose to escort the countess on the trip home, and Maddie was left to ride in rigid silence next to the earl.

Riding along watching Allie's bright head bob in laughter in response to some comment made by the viscount, Maddie became resolved on a plan that had been hatching in her brain for some time. She would go to Lady Anne's masquerade and maybe then she could settle this upset in her heart, once and for all.

Five

Maddie gave a final tug to her black domino before mounting the steps to the brightly lit town house. A gurgle of laughter almost escaped her as she thought of Marta's irate demeanor that evening. How furious she had been when Maddie demanded she search for the precious invitation to the masquerade. Her indignation had not been relieved at all when she learned that Maddie was attending the dance dressed as a man. She couldn't discern any reason for such insanity, and she had begged Maddie to drink one of her sleeping draughts and return to bed. In her estimation, all this lack of sleep had begun to turn Maddie's brain. Maddie's stronger will had prevailed, however, and now Maddie felt she was standing on the threshold of more than a crowded ballroom.

"Hello, Dennison! Over here, old man!" a boisterous voice said loudly in Maddie's ear. Maddie turned to a flushed face with drunken eyes glowing dully from behind a dark mask. She silently lifted a negating hand, causing a burst of laughter to erupt from her accoster.

"Ho, ho! Are you planning to woo the Incomparable with mystery? It won't work, Den, just won't work. How could the lady mistake that beanpole figure? Come on, Den, why spend the evening making a fool of yourself? We can get a foursome together and maybe play for interesting stakes! Wenneley is holding a table in the card room." The drunk lord took Maddie's arm and began pulling her towards the card room. Maddie shook her head furiously as she pulled backwards, causing the nobleman to stumble a bit.

"Whoa there, Den! Hold on there a minute, if you're so determined! I have half a mind to go with you! Have to keep you heading in the right direction. She's over there, you know," he added, pointing broadly. "Ach, you'll never find her in this crush. Come on, Den, I'll show you myself." With a vice-like grip on Maddie's arm he dragged her through the crowd to a knot of dominos clustered about an entrancing page boy and a delicately silvered domino.

"Good luck, Denny boy. Got to get back to Wenneley, you know. Might drink too much wine there alone!" On that note he departed, slipping awkwardly through the mass of people.

Maddie's throat was dry as she stood on the fringe of the cluster around Allie. A footman struggling to circulate with a tray of champagne glasses stopped nearby. Impulsively, Maddie lifted a glass from the tray. After a slight pause, an impish grin crossed her face and she hastily grabbed another glass from the departing tray.

It took her a few minutes to work her way to Allie's side. Allie lifted her brow when she noticed a new figure in her inner circle, and Maddie bowed gracefully.

"May I offer the ravishing Silver Domino and her page some refreshment?" she said in a low, husky voice. She presented the champagne with a flourish, taking pride in the fact that her hands were not shaking.

"What do you think, my page? Should we take gifts from a total stranger?"

"Oh la, my lady, he looks to be a comely gentleman to me! Surely such forethought speaks of a well-bred young man!"

"Then, Black Domino, I accept your offer with many thanks," said Allie, flirting gently.

"Ah, Silver Domino, ravishing star, I would have more than your thanks. Indeed, your generous nature emboldens me to request that you honor me with the next dance."

"A bold and impudent boy, Page, don't you think? Perhaps you haven't realized, sir, that the next dance is a waltz?"

"Yes, my lady, I'm aware that it's a waltz. I wouldn't waste precious time with you, letting the steps of the dance keep us apart. If I am to be granted only one dance, then I want it to be where I can gaze uninterrupted into those glorious eyes for the few, precious moments that I'll have."

"A pretty speech, my lady!" Allie's saucy page chirped in. "Beware of such a silvered tongue!"

"Hush, Page, the evening has been dull enough. I think I will bow to my vanity, and allow this young gentleman one dance for turning my head so prettily."

Allie held out her hand, which Maddie took possessively, giving it a quick squeeze before tucking it snugly into the crook of her arm. She kept her hand over Allie's as she led her out to the dance floor.

"I don't believe I recognize you, Black Domino," Allie said after a few minutes, her face flushed and her eyes sparkling with excitement.

"You are not supposed to, my lady," Maddie answered lightly. Her arms encircled Allie's waist, and she reveled in the feeling of Allie's muscles moving under her hand as they moved through the dance. In an impulsive moment she drew Allie closer, surprised to find her supple and willing.

"It's unfair for you to have the advantage of me. I feel that you know who I am."

"I would know you anywhere, Lady." Maddie's grey eyes glowed darkly from behind her mask, her voice husky with suppressed emotion.

"I think I must have met you before. There is something vaguely familiar. . ." Her voice trailed off for a moment. Suddenly, her eyes flew wide. "You!" she exclaimed.

"Yes, precious Domino. I've been unable to forget you all these long nights. I felt I could not rest until I returned these to you," said Maddie, pulling out a bulky handkerchief. "I would be grateful if you did not open it among all these curious eyes."

"My diamonds?" Allie whispered softly.

Maddie nodded slightly and was rewarded with a soft, grateful look. The moment made her feel totally devoid of reality. They whirled past long windows opening onto a balcony, and in a deft movement Maddie had whirled them out into the night air.

Allie stopped, breathless, and leaned against the rail. Unable to resist the glow of the moon in Allie's burnished gold locks, Maddie moved closer and ran her hands through Allie's thick hair. Her hands cupped Allie's face as she gently brought her lips down on Allie's. Maddie felt a deep responding chord as Allie trembled with passion. Their lips met again and Allie responded eagerly, her hands twining behind Maddie's neck as their kiss deepened.

With great decision, Maddie placed her hands on Allie's shoulders and gently set her away from her. Allie's hurt look

60

made her turn slightly away. "My love," she said softly, "we must think of your reputation. Anyone might step out and see us together, and I'm afraid, my dear, that no one would mistake your exquisite domino. You would be ruined before the night is over."

"I don't care," Allie said, her voice rough with emotion. "I want to be with you tonight. Come with me. I know a place where we can be alone." She noticed Maddie's hesitation. "Are you worried about compromising my virtue?" she continued. "You must remember that I was a married woman."

Maddie was in agony. In all her planning she had never gotten this far. How could she possibly explain this to Allie? Certainly she would lose her forever if Allie found out she was a woman.

"It is not to be, *cherie*," she said sadly, and turned to go back into the ballroom.

"I think we are destined for each other, Black Domino. Do you think that I don't know you are a woman?"

Maddie's back stiffened. Certainly now she would faint. Her legs felt weak, and the world had wrenched so on its axis. She grabbed at the doorjamb and was grateful for its reassuring solidity under her hand. She knew she couldn't turn around.

"You knew?" she asked in a barely audible whisper.

"Yes. I think I've known since our drive in the park, although it took me awhile to piece it together. Oh Maddie, I've been aware of you since the beginning. Didn't you know? You were always so controlled, though, that I didn't guess that you would return my feelings. I began to hope the night you held up my coach. There's a bond between you and I that was forged in the beginning of time. When I saw you I recognized you, even though we had never met."

"You felt that way, Allie?" Maddie turned in wonder to meet Allie's eyes. "I couldn't explain it at all. I've never believed

61

in love at first sight. I'm not sure what's going on anymore. All I know is that I can't seem to get enough of your presence and that I have a burning ache deep inside whenever I see you. I love you, Allie."

"I know, Maddie, and I love you." Allie moved close to Maddie and lifted her face invitingly. When Maddie hesitated, she put her hand behind Maddie's head and drew her lips down to her own. They stood lost in each other, drowning in long, deep kisses.

Allie finally drew back, saying, "Come, Maddie, let's go home." She grasped Maddie's hand firmly in her hers and lifted it to her lips. She planted a passionate kiss in Maddie's palm before drawing her back into the crowded ballroom.

Maddie was amazed to see everything much the same as when she left. She had felt that, somehow, everyone would be affected by the power of her and Allie's meeting on the balcony. Instead, no one seemed to have even noticed their absence.

A footman was passing by, so Maddie reached out to pluck his arm. "Please inform the page over in Lord Eaton's set that the countess has a headache and has been escorted home by an old acquaintance. And please order a hansome cab for myself."

The footman nodded and moved off through the crowd. Maddie turned to Allie. "Come, Lady, let's slip into one of these alcoves," she said, indicating small curtained niches that were sprinkled randomly along the wall.

Once inside, Maddie pulled the curtain shut behind her. "Quick, Allie, before someone comes along. Slip off your domino, and put on mine."

Allie slipped off her cloak, revealing an elegant gown of celestial blue with a silver underdress.

"You are too golden for that dress, Allie. Such beauty as yours makes silver seem dull in comparison," Maddie said with a sigh.

Allie gave her a glowing smile and slipped Maddie's domino on. With a flirtatious grin she peeped up at Maddie from under the edge of the hood, causing Maddie to forget to breathe for a moment. Catching herself, she handed Allie her black mask.

Allie twirled in front of Maddie, and Maddie chuckled as the folds of the cloak twisted around her. "A little long for you, my sweet, but it will do."

Maddie donned Allie's outfit, the shortened length allowing a glimpse of her black-clad ankles. Allie took a firm hold of Maddie's arm as they sauntered into the ballroom. Moving quickly, they wove their way to the door and escaped into the cold evening, where their cab was waiting.

They collapsed into the seat giggling with relief, and Maddie took advantage of Allie's closeness to steal a kiss.

"Not yet," Allie whispered. "Anyone could see us now!" But her eyes held a look of love and promise.

Maddie dropped Allie on her doorstep and continued in the cab for a few more blocks. She paid the driver and began to backtrack. She reached a side door of the Sifton town house and rapped softly. Her heart was racing at her own daring, and the fear of being caught. The door opened immediately, and without a word Allie led Maddie up to her bedroom.

Maddie jumped as Allie pulled the door shut behind them. Now that the moment was at hand she found her courage had deserted her, and she stood frozen.

"Come, Maddie, it's all right. I've sent my maid to bed already."

When Maddie stayed still, Allie moved close to her.

"My poor love. I forgot you have never been loved before. It's all right, my shy little dove," she murmured, and drew Maddie's head down to her shoulder.

They stood for many long moments, with Allie gently rocking Maddie back and forth, her soft arms lovingly encircling Maddie's waist.

"Oh, Allie, I'm scared. I've never done anything like this before."

"Hush, Baby, it's all right. We don't have to do anything. I just want to be close to you tonight."

Maddie lifted her head and looked searchingly into Allie's eyes. "I love you, Allie. I want to learn how to show you my love."

Allie smiled gently and raised a caressing hand to Maddie's brow. "Ah, my sweet. You show me how you love me every time your smoky eyes meet mine. I love you, sweetheart." She stepped up on her toes and kissed Maddie softly on the lips.

With a small moan Maddie crushed Allie in her arms and rained kisses on her upturned face. Her searching lips met Allie's and held them in a deep kiss. She was startled when Allie flicked her tongue across her lips, but the response of her body caused her lips to part slightly. She felt a surge in her loins as Allie's tongue slipped into her mouth to explore her honeyed sweetness.

When Allie stepped back, Maddie still had her eyes closed, reveling in the intensity of longing that was building inside her. She bowed her head to allow Allie's nimble fingers to untie the silver mask. Awkward with emotion, she slipped off Allie's mask.

She cupped her beloved's face and stared at her wonderingly. Gently she kissed Allie's eyebrows and eyelids, then trailed down each cheek, and finally brushed her lips across Allie's mouth. There she stayed for several minutes, lightly moving her lips on Allie's, exploring the soft firmness.

Allie's hands reached up to slip the domino from Maddie's shoulders. Her own quickly followed, and she pressed herself up against Maddie, igniting fires deep inside.

She led Maddie over to the bed and pressed her to sit down before moving over to the glowing fireplace. There, in the mellow red-orange light, she began slowly to undress.

Maddie was unable to turn her eyes away. She had never seen a naked woman before, and she was amazed at the beauty of the vision in front of her.

Allie turned to Maddie, her gentle roundness delicately shadowed, and began to move slowly towards her. Maddie's face was red with embarrassment and desire, and she had to use all of her self-control to remain seated. She felt the heat overcome her and wished she could escape into the safety of the night.

"Have I shocked you, love?" Allie enquired at seeing Maddie's drawn look.

Maddie, unable to speak, shook her head negatively. She finally managed to croak out, "You are beautiful, Allie."

Allie smiled saucily. "You can kiss me, Maddie. After all, I'm the same person, even without my clothes." She leaned over and kissed Maddie passionately. She planted long, loving kisses on Maddie's trembling lips until she felt the tenseness go out of Maddie's body. Then, with her lips firmly sealed on Maddie's, she pressed Maddie back down on the bed.

Maddie's arms moved gingerly to encircle Allie, and her first touch of bare skin seemed to burn her. Wonderingly, her hands moved gently up and down the smooth, taut skin on Allie's back. Allie shuddered in response and began to kiss Maddie's neck. She gently nibbled along Maddie's jaw line to her ear, where she pulled the lobe into her mouth.

Maddie lay with her eyes squeezed shut, her fingers gripping tightly to Allie's back, as she allowed her feelings to wash over her. Sometime during their lovemaking, the handkerchief that kept her hair bound tightly to her head had slipped off, and her dusky locks cascaded around her shoulders. She felt Allie unfasten her shirt, and arched up against her as Allie's mouth traveled lower and lower.

The growing ache in Maddie's breasts almost exploded as Allie circled one, then the other, with her searching tongue. A crying sob escaped Maddie as Allie's wet mouth engulfed her.

Allie was murmuring against her neck as Maddie began to regain her grasp on reality. Her hands caressed Allie, moving up to her thick locks and pulling the wondrous mouth to hers. With a deft move she rolled Allie on her back and brushed her hands gently across Allie's face. Shyly, she moved her hand down to Allie's breast, gently exploring the firm softness. Encouraged by Allie's smoky look, she flicked her thumb across one nipple and was surprised at the moan that rose on Allie's lips. Emboldened, she lowered her head to gently kiss Allie's deliciously soft skin. Her lips entrapped a rosy nipple and she held it loosely in her mouth, letting her tongue flick over it.

Allie was stirring against her, her body desperately begging for more. Maddie stopped, confused. "Allie, love, please show me what to do."

Allie's hand grasped hers and drew her fingers down to experience the musky sweetness between her legs. With a great cautiousness Maddie stroked Allie, using her gurgling moans as a guide. She felt herself stir in response to Allie's pleasure.

She paused for a moment, her mouth returning to Allie's breast. She was surprised to find Allie's hands at her waist, struggling to remove the last of the material between them. Eagerly, she moved to help.

Allie's first caressing stroke across her thigh sent Maddie spinning. With each experienced movement of those strong fingers Maddie found herself drifting farther and farther away. She rolled on her back and lay passively experiencing the glory. She gasped in wonder as she felt Allie's first burning kiss and, twining her hands in Allie's hair, she gave up her last hold on reality.

66

Time had stopped for Maddie as she lay in Allie's arms. Her skin was still tingling in the afterglow, and she felt awe at the power of what she had experienced. She remained still, dreading to lose this wonderful feeling and more than a little afraid that it was all an elaborate dream. She squeezed Allie against her to reassure herself that she was not dreaming, and Allie gently kissed her.

In a burst of love, Maddie kissed her firmly back against the pillows. Murmuring her love, she allowed her hands to roam over Allie's succulent sweetness. She closed her eyes, memorizing every inch of Allie's supple body. Her lips followed, and she felt a glow of pleasure at Allie's deepened breathing. She lowered her head to kiss Allie's inner thigh and was surprised at the heavy, musky scent. She found it exciting and began to flick her tongue against Allie's soft mound. Amazed at her own boldness, she parted Allie with her tongue and began to use broad strokes.

Allie groaned and gripped Maddie's hair. Holding her head firmly, she gently guided Maddie's searching tongue towards her center. Maddie was lost in wonder as she experimented with this new world now open to her. She was startled when Allie groaned deeply, gripped her hair painfully, and pressed her thighs together. She lay on Allie's thigh gasping for breath as Allie shuddered under her, moaning softly.

After a moment Allie reached down to draw Maddie up next to her. "Sweetheart, oh sweetheart," she murmured against Maddie's hair, and Maddie tipped her head to kiss her. They lay together, kissing and murmuring endearments to each other. It was a time of quiet magic that neither wanted to end.

For awhile they dozed, entwined, sweet sleep mixing pleasurably with the conscious sensation of touch. Maddie's senses were filled with Allie — the smell of her hair, her sweet body, her delicate taste still upon Maddie's lips. She gave a sigh of happiness and slipped off again to that place between sleep and waking.

67

She surfaced to find Allie propped on an elbow, looking down lovingly at her. She smiled and reached up to pull Allie down for a long kiss. When they came up for air, Allie rolled back to her original position, pensively tracing the lines of Maddie's face.

"What?" Maddie asked softly, almost fearfully.

"Why? Why do you do it?"

"You mean hold up coaches?"

"Yes. It's insanity to take such crazy chances for sport. It's very daring and exciting, but it's gotten so dangerous, and still you go out. Why?"

"Oh, sweet Allie," murmured Maddie, grasping Allie's hand and carrying it to her lips. "I thought you had it figured out. I don't do it for sport. I do it for necessity."

"But Maddie, why would you need to do it? You're comfortably arranged. You have the town house, and your independence!"

"I'm afraid I come from a long line of very charming spend-thrifts, Allie. Good souls all, but not a thought in their heads about money. My father was just such another, and by the time he died, what little there had been was gone. My mother, poor soul, fled creditors in London and sought refuge with some distant cousins. I'm afraid the shame of her flight and the hard new life in the country was more than she could handle, and one night she quietly passed on.

"I was desolate, but my relatives were kindhearted and jolly-natured, and I became a member of that very extended family. My mother's cousin was a local squire, so I got a tolerable education in the womanly arts, but more importantly, he was horse mad, and a strapping rider to the hounds. We discovered in each other this mutual passion in which he indulged me enthusiastically."

Maddie sighed, a distant, happy look on her face. Allie

68

waited patiently, her arm resting lovingly across Maddie's waist.

"Those were wonderful times. I miss them still. I was destined for the country as my mother was to city life. But, of course, life does not sit still, and my dearest adopted family was reaching the rough period when everybody was either getting married or demanding to be sent up to school. Oh yes, and of course Alfred, who wanted nothing more than to be bought a set of colors. It was off to follow the drum for him, and become a very famous officer. I did so envy him. But I was left to choose among a string of very dull suitors. I wanted none of them, much to the squire's wife's dismay. I was holding back my younger female cousins, because they could only afford to present one daughter, or in my case, cousin, at a time. It was a dreadful situation, and it made me quite cast down until, by happenstance, I heard my cousin regaling a neighbor with a very lively tale of a highwayman who had caused a stir in the area some thirty or forty years before. I listened eagerly to what I now realize was mostly embellishments created during the many retellings of the story. It appealed greatly to my sense of adventure, as well as being the answer to so many problems.

"I was extremely lucky on my first attempt. I bungled badly, but had the good fortune to stumble on a very timid coachman and a swooning noblewoman with a heavy purse. It encouraged me no end, and I threw myself into my new profession.

"I soon discovered the dangers of being a highway robber, and also the drawbacks of having such a limited area to work in. Soon no one traveled at night into the shire without a heavy escort, and the nobles began to make a concerted effort to catch the thief. I was forced to lie low, which greatly slowed my attempts to free myself from obligation to my cousins.

"To console my cousin's wife I feigned interest in a nobleman rusticating with relatives. I was sorry to mislead her, because she really believed she had my best interests in mind. There was no way, however, that I would marry where I was not inclined.

"To ease the pressure, I arranged to have an aunt of my dear mother 'discover' that I existed and, of course, to send a large chunk of money on my behalf. I wrote the letter myself, using the name of a crotchety old marchioness who my mother used to weave wonderfully frightening tales about."

"Maddie, you couldn't have pulled this off by yourself. Do tell who was working with you," Allie said, almost breathless.

"Well, there was Marta my maid, of course. She had been my nurse before, and since the squire already had a nurse, Marta become my maid. Two other members of my mother's staff had followed us to the shire: Henry, my groom, whom I stayed quite close to with all the time I spent in the stable; and also my butler Thompson, who had been my mother's coachman but stayed on as a gardener. Oh, how he used to grumble and complain! He's a wonderful butler, but still has lapses every once in awhile. Well, anyway, it was he who I persuaded to deliver my letter. He took himself off to visit his sick sister, but in truth headed straight for Bath. How he got the letter franked I'll never know, but he is very resourceful. He also took time while he was there to discover my marchioness aunt's direction and situation. Aunt Agatha, of course, was a true Elverton, just holding her own on the fringe of society. I felt a twinge of guilt at the elation I experienced when I heard the news. I hated to take advantage of her situation, but I was quite desperate myself.

"My cousin was puzzled when the letter arrived, and there was a great deal of wonderment and surprise, not a little unmixed with doubt and suspicion. But the squire and his wife were not about to look a gift horse in the mouth, and they presently put such thoughts behind them.

"I presently went back to robbing, although much more

70

cautiously and farther from home. In time I sent Thompson to London to procure the town house for me. I do believe he posed as my uncle, although he refused to give me the details.

"With tears in my eyes, clutching another false letter from my aunt, I bade my adopted family goodbye and went off to London, presumably on request from my aunt to join her there. I'm sure they were sorry to see me go, but I would not have been surprised or even offended if there had been a small sigh of relief at my departure.

"I traveled to London in a hired carriage, taking my few possessions and the beautiful gelding my cousin had given me as a coming out present.

"When I arrived in London, I stayed secluded in my house to avoid any damage to my reputation. I had sent a note to my aunt explaining that a trust for me from my mother's father had remained untouched until my coming of age at twenty-one. I had decided to use the small independence in London, to make my debut. I asked, very prettily, if she would have time or opportunity to come to London to act as chaperone and to bring me out to society.

"I grew quite impatient, waiting and waiting for an answering post. I felt caged knowing that she would have to answer, and then we would use the slow medium of the post to politely arrange her travel to London — *if* I was lucky enough to have her accept.

"My aunt is not a woman of half-measures, but I didn't know her at the time, or I would not have been so startled at her sudden appearance on my doorstep. I was dismayed and over-joyed by her arrival and her subsequent roughshod approach to taking everything in hand.

"As you can see, she did a marvelous job of turning me out in style, but it takes a great deal of money to maintain the façade. I returned to highway robbery to support my subsequent four years on the town. It had become increasingly obvious that I am not the marrying kind, and so I had increased my excursions to the dangerous level I am presently courting. I need the money to retire to the country that I love, Allie, and this time not only for the end of the Season. I want to find a place in the country to live. And now, more than ever, I want a place where we can be together."

Allie kissed Maddie hard, murmuring, "Yes, yes!" as she rained kisses on Maddie's upturned face. "We'll manage it somehow, Maddie, don't worry. Two heads with one goal ought to be able to turn up something!"

"Are you sure, Allie? Are you sure you want to throw your lot in with mine? We may end up in some tiny cottage with nothing else. It killed my mother, Allie, and the life we are contemplating will be much harder. Think it over before you make such a hard decision."

"Do you think I could bear this lonely life now, having loved you? I married quickly to escape London, and shed no tears when my husband broke his neck in a stupid wager. There have been other wonderful women in my heart and in my bed, but none has ever touched me like you have. No one has ever loved me with your intensity. I know that you are the one I will tie my heart to. Only you can make me happy, regardless of our surroundings."

Maddie gave a happy sigh and hugged Allie tightly to her chest. They clung together for several minutes, until Allie tipped up her chin to receive a kiss from Maddie. Kiss followed kiss, igniting their passions anew.

Allie's cool lips sent shivers of anticipation through Maddie's system as they traveled lower and lower between her breasts. Her own hands traveled up and down Allie's soft skin, caressing and exciting at the same time. Allie's deft fingers found Maddie's wet treasure, and time stopped altogether for the two lovers.

Six

Maddie sat on the edge of her bed, unable to sleep. The memory of the night burned hot in her blood, and her eyes were feverishly bright. She raised a hand to cool the high flush on her cheeks. Never before had she known such stormy passion, and she was lost in amazement at the depths of her own emotions.

She stood up and paced briskly around the room. How could the morning pass so slowly? She felt an explosion of impatience was imminent. In an attempt to control the storm, she took a deep breath and tried to compose her mind to gentle thought. She plopped herself down in a comfortable chair by the window and gazed out, with intense joy and happiness welling up inside.

She sat washed in the feeling of total rightness. Last night had erased all the doubt, fear, and confusion. Gone was the feeling of being out of step with society, that feeling of being a misfit.

The consummation of her love for Allie had taken her outside of society altogether. She saw clearly that she had never been truly a part of her culture, and that her previous unhappiness had been a result of her denial of that fact.

As she sat, she discovered a deep love for herself had sprung forth, and she hugged herself in the excitement of it. It seemed to pour out of her in all directions, and she felt like hugging the world.

A crooked grin formed on Maddie's lips. She really must get a hold of herself! If she floated down the stairs and planted a loud kiss on her aunt's cheek, they'd probably try to keep her confined to her room for the entire day! She couldn't risk her plans to meet Allie in the park in such a foolish way.

She sighed. So much wasted time. Her endless years on the town; Allie's sad years of marriage. Allie's deep sorrowful eyes as she talked about her marriage haunted Maddie, and her voice had been bitter.

It had been Aunt Constance, whom Allie loved dearly even while resenting her painful interference, who had brought Allie to London for her come out. She had pressed Allie into marriage, arguing that it opened so many doors closed to a single woman. After she had born her husband an heir or two she could be free to carry on, discreetly of course, as she wished.

Allie's self-centered husband had become brutish and mean after they were wed, and she had found it hard to talk about that period of agony. His cruelty had been especially hard for Allie to deal with, for she had already known the sweetness of another woman. To Allie's heartfelt relief, her husband's drinking and gambling kept him away from home more often than not, and she would have danced in the streets during his funeral if it hadn't been for Lady Sifton.

They had talked further about Aunt Constance, unable to fathom her present goal in bringing Allie to London. "Not marriage this time!" Allie had said emphatically. She was through with men and had only one woman on her mind. Maddie had been deeply moved by this pronouncement, and the two had tumbled back on the bed for some arduous lovemaking.

Maddie smiled to herself. How she wished she could have slept there with her own true love. Much too soon the night had ended, and she had had to creep silently home. Marta had said nothing, convinced that Maddie had compromised her virtue, and had left Maddie to meditate on her sinfulness. Maddie had almost laughed out loud as the door closed behind her.

† † † † †

Maddie lifted a hand to her stylish hat before gathering up her gloves and riding crop from the mantle in front of her. She draped the extra length of her skirt over one arm and sailed elegantly out to her waiting mount. She shot a look of impish devilry at Thompson, who was holding the door, and regally nodded to Henry after he handed her into the saddle. He gave her a broad wink. She gave a final tug to her crisply tailored riding jacket and arranged her skirts around her as Henry mounted his hack to escort her to the park.

Maddie's horse danced and spooked as they wound their way through the streets of London. Maddie's eagerness and excitement were being clearly communicated to the sensitive steed beneath her, and the mare shied at all manners of unseen danger, demanding Maddie's full attention.

She was taking exception to a large rumbling wagon as they arrived at the park entrance, and it was with great relief that Maddie turned her into the safety of the rolling greens. She allowed her a brief canter in the grassway alongside the main drive. As the park was still fairly empty, Henry held back his word of censure.

Maddie made her way quickly to where Allie waited on her dainty mare. Allie reined her horse out onto the path and drew alongside Maddie. With a careless gesture she signaled her groom back with Henry, who was following at a respectful distance.

"Good morning, Maddie!" Allie said warmly, reaching out a hand to briefly grasp Maddie's forearm.

"Isn't it glorious!" Maddie responded, her voice alive and vibrant with feeling. "I couldn't wait to come and see you again. I had this nonsensical urge to abandon Aunt Agatha to her stuffy breakfast and come immediately to the park. I felt the hours would be easier to bear here, somehow, but I was very good and managed to stay rooted to my chair long enough to satisfy my aunt. I know I'm being horribly silly!"

"And wonderfully romantic!" Allie finished. "I was half-afraid you wouldn't come today, that last night wasn't real, or that you would regret it."

"Silly," Maddie said affectionately, her eyes resting softly on Allie's countenance. "I love you. Obviously, you must get to know me better! Of course, tonight I am attending a dinner with my aunt. I would complain of a headache, but she's on the brink of whisking me away from London as it is. She's afraid I'm too tired lately! I just couldn't bear it if I had to be away from you!"

"At least now we can see each other during the day," Allie said, nodding her head in agreement. "I think we should take up my aunt's suggestion. You could teach me how to drive. It would give you an excellent excuse to sit close to me and occasionally place your hands over mine!" Allie's coy smile dipped from view as she gave her reins an intensive study.

Maddie gave a low chuckle. "The pleasure would be mine, my lady. Shall I pick you up at Lady Sifton's tomorrow? We'd make quite a dashing turnout."

"That would be wonderful! I must warn you that I'm already a passable whip. All I need is a little polish, a little of your flare."

"An easy accomplishment. Is that the only way I'm going to get to know you better?" Maddie gave Allie an arch look.

"There is one thing."

"Yes?"

"Maddie, did you used to go out robbing after your evening engagements? Like tonight, would you usually have gone out?"

"Well, yes. It was the only way. And tonight would have been perfect, little moon."

"Let's do it then. Let's hold up a coach tonight!"

Maddie's sudden movement caused her horse to hesitate, and Maddie was forced to urge her forward so the grooms would not overtake them.

"Are you daft? What can you be thinking of? With the lieutenant and his army of men out to hang me from the highest tree, you want me to risk you like this?"

"Oh, come on, Maddie! They'll think we did it for a lark! They'll slap our wrists and send us home, naughty children that we are. The marchioness has enough influence to pull us out of this scrape. But we won't get caught! Just once, and I'll never ask you again. I need to know what it's like. Maybe I wouldn't worry about you so much if I knew how you managed it. You might as well take me, or I'll do it myself!"

"Allie Sifton, you are the most stubborn creature I've ever met. What has come over you?"

"I plan to go out tonight and hold up a carriage, Magdalena, with or without you. Are you coming?"

Maddie heaved a sigh and gave a shrug of her shoulders. "Allie, my love, I can't let you go alone, and I wish more than anything that you would reconsider. It is very dangerous. But if your mind is set, I have no choice. I will go to keep you from getting yourself killed. Now, listen to me . . . ."

† † † † †

Maddie paced back and forth in the clearing where she and Allie were to meet. She slapped her gloved hands together, encouraging them not to lose their feeling. Her breath rose in a frosty cloud in the crisp night air. The ground was soft under her feet. Not long now and it would be covered with snow, Maddie thought idly. Where was Allie?

There! Finally. She could hear the sounds of Allie's approach. Quickly she mounted and moved to meet Allie on the path.

Her first glimpse of her beloved brought tears of laughter to Maddie's eyes.

"Oh, don't laugh, Maddie! Where was I to get boys' clothes in such a hurry?"

"You make an adorable stable boy!" Maddie answered, riding up and planting a resounding kiss on Allie's lips. Fabian stood patiently, although he pinned his ears at Allie's mount. The antiquated gelding ignored this insult entirely, having no time for young upstarts.

"Looks like you stole his cob, too!" Maddie continued with a grin.

"Not stole, heftily bribed. Don't worry about this old charger. I have been informed that he was a demon in his time. I'm sure he'll do nicely, and at least he won't be given to nervous starts!" Allie ended with a twinkle.

Maddie laughed, her face alive with the joy of being out of the city and in the presence of her love. Love radiated outwards in all directions, and Allie gave Maddie a studying look.

"We must move to the country soon," she said decisively.

Maddie gave her a startled look. "Well, yes, of course. As soon as we can."

"It has to be very soon. I never realized how much the city drains you." Allie lifted a hand to Maddie's face. "You should always be this alive. The city is killing you, Maddie. We must get you out."

Maddie grasped Allie's hand and raised it to her lips, the love shining in her eyes. "We must get to the road now. Here, take this pistol. Careful now, it's ready to fire."

"I've never handled a gun before," Allie said timidly.

"Just do as we planned. You won't even have to fire it."

"All right. Lead on!"

The two made their way to the edge of the woods. Allie shifted excitedly in her saddle as they waited for a coach to approach. "So brazen, to be riding astride," she whispered, and was hushed by Maddie.

At last there were sounds of a coach moving steadily towards them. Allie glanced at Maddie, who answered with a nod. Allie pulled down her silver mask, left from the masquerade, and tugged the large-brimmed hat farther down on her forehead. Maddie's eyes were bright with amusement, but she said nothing.

Both were gathered and ready now. Allie had a fierce expression on her face, and the pistol held gingerly in her hand. Even her horse seemed to have awakened enough to experience the occasion.

The coach was almost abreast of them now, and Maddie raised her hand, ready to signal Allie to follow her. The moment must be just right.

Suddenly, Allie burst past her with a loud whoop, her aged mount alive with the excitement of the moment. Maddie was slow in signaling her gelding after them, confusion and concern being topmost in her mind.

She was on Allie's heels when the intrepid lady fired her pistol and bellowed a loud "Stand, and deliver!"

For Maddie, the whole situation was now totally out of control. Allie had succumbed to the fever of the moment, and somehow she had to salvage the situation.

With a snarl she aimed her pistol at the coachman, who was preparing to leap on the unsuspecting Allie.

"No foolish heroics," she snapped, and was relieved when the able young gentleman sank back onto his perch.

She turned her attention back to Allie, who had managed to open the carriage door from horseback. The patient cob stood quietly as Allie struggled to regain an upright position on his back.

"Step down, sirs!" Allie growled fiercely.

"Look, Peter, it's a boy. Surely the coachman can just drive on?" a voice emanated from the carriage.

"Step down, I said!" Allie's pitch was climbing.

"I can't see why. This is very tiresome. Signal the coachman to move on, Peter. I'll catch the death of a cold sitting in this night air."

"You're not going anywhere until you step down and hand over your valuables."

Maddie rode over to add her own imposing figure to Allie's. She rested her weight forward on her horse's neck, the cocked pistol held carelessly, but with deadly accuracy.

"Perhaps you will oblige us, sirs. The boy grows impatient." Maddie's even voice was formidable, her face set. Her eyes twinkled coldly from behind her mask.

Without a word the two gentlemen stepped out onto the road.

Two of the dandy set, Maddie thought with a sneer, disgusted at their foppish apparel.

Allie, feeling her confidence returning, held out an imperative hand. "Your purses, please. And that beautiful diamond at your throat. Ah, thank you. And, Peter, is it? That is a beautiful ring. Would you mind terribly?"

80

Peter's face was twisted with rage, but the pistol was turned steadily on him and he reluctantly obliged.

"Thank you, sirs!" Allie said brightly, and turned to Maddie. A jerk of Maddie's head signaled Allie's departure and, after her beloved had had time to safely escape, Maddie turned to follow.

They both reached the clearing together, and Maddie tumbled from her horse. Tears ran down her face, and her chest heaved with suppressed mirth.

"Stand and deliver," she growled, and dissolved into boisterous laughter.

Allie stood disapprovingly over her for a moment before she, too, joined in the laughter and plopped herself down next to Maddie.

"Wasn't it ridiculous? But so thrilling. I *felt* like a highwayman, charging down on the unsuspecting coach. I'm afraid I was lost in the moment."

"Yes, and almost got yourself into a bit of trouble!"

"Ah, bah! You were there, you old sourpuss. They would've listened to me if I hadn't already fired my pistol. But I must say, my dear, I do like your style. So cold. So calculating. Did it take a great deal of practice?"

"Some. Come, my pet. We must get home. My Marta is quite used to this sort of kick-up, but your maid'll be half out of her mind, if my past experience with Marta is any indication!"

"I'm too excited to go home. How will I ever sleep? What will I do with my spoils?"

"Give them to me. I've got a very efficient system for fencing little gew-gaws. That's the way. Now mount up."

"No."

"No?"

"Not until you kiss me. Really, you forget everything that is important when..."

Maddie's lips cut off any further comments, and the two

spent a few agreeable moments exchanging passionate kisses and murmuring little nothings.

"Tomorrow is such a long way away," Allie groaned. "How will I wait? I'll go insane!"

"I know, my sweet," said Maddie, dropping a kiss on Allie's brow. "But then we'll have so much more time. We *must* go. Every moment puts us more in danger of being discovered by your lieutenant. We must reach London before our dandies reach him. He has the capability of covering all the roads into London!"

Allie sighed. "I know," she said, moving to mount her horse. "Until tomorrow, my darling!"

"I'm escorting you home. How could I sleep, knowing you might be in trouble?" Maddie said passionately.

"Only to that section of town, Maddie. You know we'd be safer apart then."

Maddie nodded reluctantly, and the two rode off together.

† † † † †

The sun shone brightly through the bay windows in the front sitting room as Maddie paced restlessly, oblivious to the cheery sight. Occasionally she stopped to peer out to the court below, willing her groom to appear with her carriage.

For awhile she stood at the window, idly pulling her gloves through her hand, her tall figure imposing in the dove grey outfit she had chosen for this morning's drive. The pleasure she had felt earlier in her appearance was lost in the impatience she was experiencing now.

What if something had happened to Allie? Had she made it home safely after the two of them had departed? Had she been found out by her aunt?

Maddie lifted a steadying hand to her head. She had studied these questions relentlessly all through the night, and she was anxious to see Allie and put her fears to rest. If only Henry would appear.

She moved from the window and had resumed her steady pacing, when the sound of carriage wheels on the cobblestones caught her ear. With two long strides she reached the window, relieved to see that it was indeed Henry.

In no time she had bolted down the stairs and out the door. She gained the seat of the phaeton easily and signaled her groom to step away from her horse's head. She gave her horse office to start, causing Henry to scramble to his perch as the carriage bowled out of the courtyard.

Maddie moved the phaeton along at a fast clip, her attention focused on threading her way quickly through the congestion of the London streets. She was oblivious to everything except her arrival on Allie's doorstep.

Maddie breezed up to Lady Sifton's town house, stopping smartly as Allie fluttered down the steps to meet her. She smiled as Allie daintily waited for Henry to hand her up, amused at her love's air of nonchalance. A sharp signal to Henry to wait for her here, and the carriage was gone, continuing its breathless trip to the park.

"Oh, Allie. I was so worried! You had no problems?" Maddie asked at last.

"None whatsoever, unless you count not being able to sleep a wink!"

"I know. Sheer torture! And then, morning callers," Maddie finished with a groan. She pulled herself stiffly upright, taking care not to job her horse's mouth, and made a long face.

"The Howard-Jameses to see you, Madam. The Lady Anne Billingsly, Madam," Maddie said, her voice remarkably similar to her butler's. "It must've gone on for hours. Smiling, speaking prettily, turning a polite comment. It seems ironic that the *ton*, with its extreme dislike of actors and such, would require every member of its elite corps to be more talented than any who have ever trod the boards!"

"Maybe you should consider it as an alternative career,"

Allie responded, her voice full of fun.

"I think not! My reputation and, I'm afraid, my pride could not tolerate such a blow. I would not like to be *shunned* by the *ton*, just ignored by it. Besides, there's a bit of pleasure in tweaking their noses. Couldn't do that if I weren't a vicious highwayman."

"Vicious," Allie humphed. "I, on the other hand, had an extremely interesting visitor this morning."

"Yes?" Maddie answered, her attention being distracted by the turn into the park.

"Lt. Bridgewater called."

Maddie made a small sputtering sound but kept her thoughts to herself.

"I believe his frustration has forced him to go out again. He really is quite startling in appearance, with his angry red scar across his cheek. How in the world did you manage to do that?"

"I panicked, and hit him with the butt of my pistol. I realized at the time that I had done more damage than I had intended, but what was done was done, and I abandoned him. I do not consider myself a violent person, and it was never my intention to do more than knock him unconscious."

"After last night, I think I understand that desperation. It is a problem, though. Hand over the reins, my dear, and I will fill you in."

Maddie gladly relinquished the reins. She felt tired, and unable to cope at the moment with the thought of the lieutenant. She was glad for Allie's breezy decisiveness and listened intently, interrupting only to make minor corrections in Allie's driving.

"I was sitting in the garden when the lieutenant was announced, and I was a great deal more startled than you have indicated you were!" Allie said, her voice tending towards the indignant.

"I am, however, the mistress of my emotions..."

Maddie snorted, but was silenced by Allie's black look.

"...and by the time he had entered the garden I was prepared for the worst. Not being one to wait for fate to find me, I fluttered solicitously forward. You would have been quite proud.

"He was being very correct, and all the while his eyes smouldered with anger. I felt such a great relief when I realized that he had not come to charge me with being a robber, and in fact had absolutely no reason to even suspect me in the first place, that I played the role of the confidant with a great deal more sympathy than usual.

"The lieutenant, as always, was highly responsive to shameless flattery, and in a very short time he was speaking freely to me.

"I'm afraid, Maddie, that the search for you has become a personal vendetta for him, and in some twisted way he believes it is the same for you. He believes that you held me up that night to get even with him — that the other carriages you held up that night were simply an attempt to locate my coach!"

"This is totally ridiculous!" Maddie exclaimed. "I can't believe it! Why in the world would a highwayman care about the lieutenant? I wouldn't have known who he was if you hadn't been kind enough to let on the first time we went for a drive." Maddie gave Allie's wrist a light squeeze, the fondness of that memory overwhelming her initial amazement.

"You must remember that the lieutenant has an exaggerated focus on himself. And while the man is intelligent, his thinking circles around Lt. Michael Bridgewater. He puts himself in your shoes and decides what he would do. *Voila*, his motives become yours. Simple!"

"But even if we follow his thinking, how would a common thief be aware of his actions? The *ton* does guard its elite ranks pretty closely."

85

"That, Maddie, is where we may have run into some trouble. I told you before that the lieutenant believes that the highwayman may, in fact, be a woman."

"Or a boy, you said. But even if he were correct about the thief being a woman, that is hardly narrowing in a place like London." Maddie's tone was bordering on smug.

"Your cultured accent did not go unnoticed, sweetheart. That would make you a woman of quality," Allie countered.

"So? A young nobleman down from school would cut such a lark."

"It's more complicated than that. The lieutenant discovered the clearing where we met. The ground was cut up a bit from our horses, but he managed to find a few distinct footprints from your pacing. Woman-sized feet."

"But boys have small feet, and . . ."

"For Lt. Bridgewater they are a woman's bootprints, and there is no changing that in his mind. He believes that my appearance as a stable boy was a simple ruse to throw him off the scent. Female trickery is what I believe he called it, excepting present company, of course."

Maddie was silent, frantically trying to absorb and assess this new threat.

"At present there is no need to panic," Allie continued. "The lieutenant has not had time to use the information to focus his suspicions. He is, at this moment, trying to recall everyone with whom he has confided. As a victim, I am above suspicion, but it was difficult to dissuade him from interrogation of the Dowager Thornapple. I also managed to divert certain disaster when he decided it was Alexandra Dinwiddie he should lock up!"

"I would have loved to have seen that!" Maddie said with an irreverent giggle. "But I'm afraid it'll never happen to her. Her dearest papa is far too powerful in Parliament to take such a chance with."

"But Michael is insane with this, Maddie! It did absolutely no good to point out such lucid details! He felt that station or wealth should not protect the perpetrator. He waxed elegant on this score. I'm afraid one day he will go too far, and although he is not the most charming man of my acquaintance, I'm sure I don't want to see him come into a bad way. What if they have him locked up?"

Maddie threw back her head and laughed heartily. "Maybe that's what he needs!"

"Oh, Maddie. He's not insane. Both you and I know that! In fact he's figured it out most admirably! No, no you're too cruel! Don't make me laugh! It's really not funny!"

But it was too late, and the two dissolved into a fit of giggles. They were laughing still when Maddie glanced up.

"Oh no!" she muttered in dismay, cutting through Allie's chuckles. "I can't believe it! Lord Edmund!" she ended with a groan.

"The Earl of Alvon? But why the sour face, Maddie?"

"Maybe you've noticed the coolness between us?"

"Well, of course, at the outing there seemed to have been some distance between you, but I thought he was sulking over the Viscount Perry's attention to you!"

"It's much more than that, Allie! Do you remember the first night we saw each other?"

"Vividly," Allie answered with a sigh. "You were so shy!" she added fondly.

Maddie's colour was heightened as she continued. "I punched him, and he fell into the pond." Her voice was sulky.

Allie's mouth formed a delicate O, and her eyes were wide as she looked at Maddie with an expression of amazement, and not a little envy. "Maddie!" she squeaked.

"Well, he tried to kiss me and quite mauled me in the process. There was very little of the gentleman about him then!"

"But in the pond!"

"A fountain really, and it was his fault anyway. I only punched him! He was the one who lost his balance!"

"How hard did you hit him? Never mind, I don't even want to know! I know I should reprimand you or something, but personally I feel you should be applauded!"

Maddie opened her mouth to hotly defend herself, but was forced instead to give a nod of greeting to Lord Edmund as he drew level with them.

"Good day, Lord Edmund," Allie said elegantly, drawing up the phaeton.

The earl's well-bred manners forced him to also stop. "Good day, Countess, Miss Elverton," the earl returned formally.

"I just wanted to thank you for a most entertaining outing, Lord Edmund. I don't believe I've had a more enjoyable day since I've returned to London."

Allie's admiring tones had a strong effect on the earl, and he warmed considerably under her gaze.

"It was my pleasure, my lady. I may add that an outing is destined to be enjoyable when your presence graces it," the earl said, his sense of the dramatic rising visibly to the fore.

Allie smiled shyly, causing Maddie to feel a surge of jealousy. This was followed by a strong urge to strangle Allie on the spot.

At that moment Allie turned her head slightly to Maddie and gave her a discreet wink. Maddie raised an eyebrow but gave no indication of her feelings.

"Miss Elverton and I are planning to attend Almack's tonight. Will we see you there?" Allie enquired of the earl.

"I shall make it a point to attend."

"Very good. We shall look forward to meeting you. Good day." Allie gave her horse office to start, leaving Lord Edmund with a satisfied look on his face.

"There," Allie said with satisfaction. "Now he will not go

around like a storm cloud whenever he sees us. See how lucky you are? You have a wonderfully correct lover who will protect you from all social slights!"

Allie batted her eyelashes at Maddie and Maddie's spasm of jealousy dissolved. She gave Allie a warm loving look, and a happy smile danced across her face.

"You devilish imp! I do love you so!" Maddie said, her voice soft with emotion.

"And I you, my pet! But the park is filling, and it's not safe to continue in this very enjoyable strain. Perhaps I can coax you into visiting me tonight?" Allie's voice was coy.

"Is there anything that could stop me?" Maddie returned.

The two made their way slowly from the park, stopping often to greet acquaintances. This was a part of society Maddie would in no way miss when she said goodbye to London.

Seven

Maddie sat in the drawing room with her aunt, receiving morning callers. She sat quietly, listening to the drone of conversation, glad that there was no attempt to draw her into it. Her smile was soft, but a closer inspection revealed eyes that were vacant. The largest part of Maddie's attention was turned inward.

She focused idly on the butler as he appeared in the doorway, wondering in a vague way about who would be announced.

"The Countess Fawnhope."

Maddie's attention sharpened and she was able to rise gracefully to welcome Allie into the room. Greetings were exchanged, and Maddie easily drew Allie aside.

"Hello, Allie." Maddie's voice was careful but her eyes were warm. "It was good of you to come. Perhaps now I will finally have the opportunity to show you my stable. I am unbecomingly proud of my horses!"

"It would be a pleasure," Allie answered.

Maddie turned and excused them to her aunt, mentioning that they were off to tour the stable.

"Oh Maddie," Lady Agatha sighed.

"I have developed quite an interest in Maddie's horses since she has been teaching me how to drive," Allie cut in quickly, her smile bright and her voice coaxing. "I've finally talked Maddie into sharing her knowledge of horses with me."

"My dear, horses are a passion for Magdalena. Be forewarned that any encouragement in this area, and you might find yourself unable to check the resulting outpour." Lady Elverton's voice held an affectionate warning, but an offhand wave dismissed them.

They exited in silence, saving their words until they were past the range of any curious ears. Maddie's head was full of questions. Although the two had not seen each other for days, every night had been spent in the other's company, and there had been no mention of Allie coming to call.

"What are you doing here?" Maddie hissed as they stepped out into the courtyard.

"Coming to see you, love," Allie answered brightly. "Surprised?"

"An understatement. Has something happened?"

"Don't be in a fuss. It's good news, or I would have swept you off so we would have more time. No matter. Lt. Bridgewater called again this morning to unburden himself to his sole friend and confidant. I was charming, as usual."

"I thought you said this was good news," Maddie groaned.

"Actually, it is very good news. The road to Bath will be unguarded tonight. The lieutenant is livid. I gathered from his rantings that there is some rich crusty nobleman traveling from London by that route, but the lieutenant's men are to be stationed elsewhere to guard a large movement of government money. He is at this moment trying to convince this lord to hire some sort of protection, but I understand the man keeps very tight purse strings."

"Allie, this is wonderful!" Maddie exclaimed, her arm encircling Allie's waist and whirling her around.

"Maddie, really!"

A hasty glance about failed to reveal observers. Still, the two continued more cautiously.

"You'll go, then?" Allie enquired.

"Yes, of course, this should be the answer to our dreams. Where will you be? I won't be able to sleep until I share this with you."

"And until *I* know you are safe! I will be at Almack's tonight with my aunt, and I have very cleverly gotten the lieutenant to escort me. Not a small feat, I may add. Be careful, Maddie. And be aware that Lt. Bridgewater will be watching everyone with suspicious eyes."

"Have faith. I'm an old hand at this! Come on. You really must meet Fabian in the daylight!"

Maddie was delighted at Allie's appreciation of her equine friends. At last she had found someone with whom she could share her passion completely. Time flew by as she talked about her horses and she was surprised, and saddened, when it was time for Allie to leave.

Maddie pressed Allie's hand warmly before Allie stepped into the waiting carriage and gave a small disconsolate wave as she pulled away. Only the thought of being reunited with her love that evening consoled her, and she was even more resolved to find a way for the two of them to be together always.

Maddie went upstairs for a brief rest before she would join her aunt. Before she lay down, however, she scribbled off a hasty letter to Charles requesting that he escort her to Almack's that night. She had a whim to arrive late, she added, but reminded him that the doors closed at precisely at 11:00. Did he think he could make it? They would, after all, make a very dashing couple.

Maddie went to her room as soon as the letter was safely entrusted to a footman, not bothering to wait for an answer. She knew that the viscount could never refuse a lark.

At tea she informed her aunt that she was attending an impromptu dinner with friends, from which Lord Delvin would then escort her to Almack's. Dear Helen's mother had agreed to act as chaperone, so Aunt Agatha would be free to spend a relaxing evening at home, if she wished.

Lady Elverton's doubts were laid to rest by the mention of Mrs. Latham, and she cheerfully saw Maddie off that evening in their own coach.

Maddie lay back against the cushions with a sigh of relief. Aunt Agatha had forgotten it was the coachman's night off, or she would never have let her go out with only Henry as an escort. The whole affair had been a series of bluffs, and she had managed to play it masterfully.

Henry would drop her at the edge of town, where he had hid her gelding. He would wait there for her to return, and with time being of the essence he would then take her to the viscount's door. This was a daring move, and very risky, with her aunt's coat of arms clearly emblazoned on the doors of the coach. Any passing observer could make things uncomfortable for Maddie, as a woman simply did not visit a gentleman at his own residence. Maddie, of course, had the excuse of the viscount being late for her aunt, but her reputation was already tenuous in the eyes of society.

Henry pulled the carriage to a stop and handed Maddie down. She required Henry's help in getting out of her elegant gown, much to that young man's chagrin. But Maddie was brisk and businesslike about the whole episode and soon galloped away from the blushing groom, who stood gingerly holding her undergarments.

Maddie traveled quickly to her selected place for the rendezvous. She pulled irately at the hood of the cape that threatened to slip back and reveal the elegant coiffure beneath. There had been no way to bind her hair to her head tonight. Without Marta, or even a mirror, she could never have gotten it piled so neatly upon her head. Maddie shrugged to herself, resigned to the risks of the situation.

Soon enough the sound of a ponderous coach carried to Maddie's ears. She gathered her horse beneath her and watched as the carriage pulled into view. At the point of hurling down the slope to the road, Maddie suddenly checked her horse. Fabian flicked his ears in confusion but remained still. "Outriders!" Maddie spat the word out in her mind. Of course, the old crustacean had hired four outriders to escort him.

Maddie huddled into her cape in disgust as the coach passed serenely. She sat on her horse trying to decide if she had time to wait for another victim, when the sound of another coach could be heard. From the sounds it made as it bounced and jostled across the road, the coachman was pushing his horses at an insane pace. Maddie smiled at her private thoughts. It was her duty to stop this coach, if only to save the poor passenger from being rattled to death.

With that thought she burst onto the road, firing her pistol. She sent up a thankful prayer that the horses were so tired, for even as it was they threatened to spook into the yawning ditch at the far side of the road.

With a fluid motion Maddie swung open the door of the

carriage and drew her horse back a few steps. She watched in amazement as an aged man of indeterminate years levered himself out of the carriage and stood unsteadily before her. His grey hair shone in the light of the carriage lanterns, and one gnarled hand rested on an ornate cane.

With a disappointed sigh she dismounted and wordlessly held out her hand in front of the gentleman. Her unfired pistol was steady in her grasp. The passenger reached into his pocket and withdrew his purse. Without a word or glimmer of expression he placed it in Maddie's hand.

Maddie's eyes widened with surprise at the weight of the purse, and she quickly dropped her head to hide her amazement. She tucked the bag away and raised her eyes to reassess her victim.

The old man stood unmoving, leaning weakly on his cane. He was dressed plainly and wore no ornamentation, not even a signet ring. Maddie's eyes stared into his and found a steely resistance. His unbending look gave her no clues to his thoughts.

Maddie turned to examine the interior of the carriage and carelessly thrust her pistol into her belt. Her searching hands quickly discovered the compartment under the seat, and with a gurgle of triumph she pulled a large leather pouch from under the seat. She tucked the bag under her belt as she turned, and froze in place.

There, inches from her face, was a wicked blade held in an unwavering hand. A swordstick! Maddie thought in disgust. A replica from the past.

Her mind refused to work rationally. Over and over she wondered why she hadn't heard him slip the cane off the blade. She drew a long breath and took her eyes and mind off the glittering steel. She raised her eyes to those of the old gentleman's, and forced her body to relax from its rigid stance.

She stood balanced and loose, her body ready to move in any direction she demanded.

"You are an impudent dog," the old man growled, "but a foolish one. They told me you were a fox, maybe even the devil, but you're not smart enough to outwit me!"

The old man gave a crackling chuckle.

Maddie stood silent, willing the old man to drop the point slightly. As it was, it wavered before her eyes, threatening her delicate features. The light of the carriage lantern behind her glittered in the eyes of the gentleman, giving him a look of cold competence. She had underestimated him because of his age; a lesson for her.

"Lt. Bridgewater seems to be in some awe of you. Wanted me to hire outriders! The man's a fool. A total incompetent. Should've caught you a long time ago. Anyone with sense would've!"

Maddie felt a start of surprise. So this had been the lieutenant's crusty nobleman after all! Her lip curled at the irony of it.

"Perhaps now you'll hand over the pistol, eh, lad? That's a good boy. I'll take my money, too, if you please."

Maddie carefully handed over her pistol, not wanting to startle the old man. The pouch and purse followed.

"Now turn around slowly, and we'll bind you up," the nobleman continued, his voice filled with glee.

As he spoke he dropped the point of the blade to Maddie's chest to give her room to move. This was the break Maddie had been waiting for. She began to turn slowly, and with amazing speed spun back, deflecting the flat of the blade with her gloved hand and bringing her other fist around in a roundhouse that caught the nobleman squarely on the chin.

The force of Maddie's blow was enough to knock him to the ground, and without further thought she leaped on top of him. Desperately, she pinned his sword arm to the ground while frantically digging in his pocket for her pistol.

Her panic subsided as she realized he was lying unresisting under her. Calmer now, she managed to recover not only her pistol, but both purses.

She stood up panting, the pistol steady in her grasp. The old man lay propped up on one elbow, managing, somehow, to maintain his air of dignity and pride.

Maddie remained undecided for a few moments, staring into that sad and tired face. In an impulsive gesture, she tossed the smaller purse at the nobleman's feet and whirled around to quickly remount Fabian.

Maddie put her heels to her horse and sprinted off to the woods. She chastised herself for being such a soft-hearted fool as she wended her way back to the carriage.

"Miss Maddie," Henry started in a fearful whisper, "how long has your hood been back like that?"

Maddie lifted a distressed hand to her hair and groaned aloud. It would have been impossible to miss the riot of dark curls in the light from the carriage lanterns. Had it been back when she stopped the old man? Was he observant enough to have noticed?

Maddie brushed such thoughts aside, having no time for futile worrying. There was nothing she could do about it now anyway. She would take a page from Aunt Agatha's book, and bluster her way through.

Climbing back into her ball gown without Marta was even more difficult than shedding it had been. The occasional glimpses of Henry's embarrassed face, however, allowed her to maintain her sense of humor, and her temper. Both gave a long sigh of relief when Maddie was finally bundled into the carriage.

Maddie was glad to rest against the cushions and allow Henry to handle matters for a time. She did sit up nervously as he ran up to the viscount's door, but the street seemed com-

97

pletely deserted. Still, Maddie was unable to relax until Lord Delvin was seated inside and the carriage was moving sedately towards Almack's.

"Maddie, what insanity is this? Is it true? Are you finally abducting me?"

"Oh Charles! I was simply afraid you would be late!"

"You malign me," said the viscount in injured tones. "How did Marta let you escape with that errant curl threatening to ruin the effect of that elegant coiffure? Here, let me tuck it up. No fear now. I promise not to ruin the whole. Maddie, you madcap, I know you're up to something, but I promise not to expose you."

"That's very good of you, but nothing is going on! I have a strand of hair out of place, and you immediately suspect me of who knows what! Really, Charles!"

The viscount gave her a long look but kept his peace. His doubts began to seem ridiculous as he engaged Maddie in spirited light banter. In no time they had reached the doors of the hallowed Almack's.

Maddie stole a quick look in the long mirror as she and the viscount were announced. Satisfied with her appearance, she sailed into the ballroom on Charles's arm.

From a corner, surrounded by young swains, Allie signaled to Maddie. Maddie answered with a nod and requested that the viscount take her to join her friend.

"Hello, Maddie!" Allie greeted her, shifting over on the bench to make room for her to sit. "Have you had a good evening?" she enquired, lifting an eyebrow.

"Yes, I've had a very enjoyable time. Everything went better than expected!" she added with a light laugh.

She continued talking to Allie, her spirited conversation hiding nervousness. Quick, upward glances under her eyelashes allowed her to observe the long inspection Lt. Bridgewater gave her. He continued to stare disconcertingly at her, his raw scar showing brightly on his cheek. Just before Maddie was about to give herself away with a self-conscious movement or an ill-placed word, the lieutenant's attention made a sudden shift to another woman across the room.

Maddie almost giggled in relief and watched with no small enjoyment as Lt. Bridgewater thoroughly inspected the female persons in the room. Some he obviously dismissed, and others he observed for long uncomfortable minutes.

Later, when Allie and Maddie retired to freshen themselves, Maddie overheard several women discussing the lieutenant's strange behavior. Maddie saw it as a point in her favor if he ever landed on her as the identity of the infamous highway robber.

Maddie was able to relax and enjoy the evening. Both she and Allie danced the night away, always coming back to each other to rest or enjoy some refreshment. Maddie even stood up once with Lord Edmund, who behaved very decorously. Both women were sorry to see the evening end, and as they were taking leave of each other, Maddie asked Allie to join her for a drive the next day. She would be glad to teach Allie the art of looping a rein. Allie accepted prettily and was ushered out to her waiting carriage.

Maddie and Charles followed, and Maddie was relieved when the viscount was dropped at his door. She reached under the seat to the hidden compartment and pulled out the heavy purse stashed there. She gave a little squeak as she opened it. There, filled almost to overflowing, was a brilliant array of rubies, diamonds, emeralds, and sapphires. She gathered up a handful of the glittering stones. Here in her grasp was the means to obtaining a delicious future with Allie. It would take time to exchange them without arousing suspicion, but soon enough they would be free! She would tell Allie tomorrow. When I'm driving, Maddie thought with a gurgle of laughter, or more likely than not they would end up overturned!

† † † † †

Maddie tooled her phaeton towards the Marchioness of Quinton's residence to pick up her beloved Allie. Henry squeaked from his perch behind her as she slipped through an impossibly narrow gap between an overloaded wagon and a ponderous barouche. His subsequent monologue communicated his disapproval of such unwarranted haste. Maddie ignored him completely, as a large part of his speech was unfit for delicately nurtured ears.

Marta had felt strongly enough last night to deliver a similar speech after Maddie had shown her the magnificent booty she had stolen. Maddie had danced around her while Marta muttered such words as "reckless" and "insane." But even sour Marta had smiled, although only slightly, when Maddie had swung her around proclaiming that her thieving days were over! It had taken some time to convince Marta that the jewels could be fenced gradually, but Maddie knew she had won when Marta murmured something about retiring to her own cottage.

Maddie was smiling vaguely when Henry gave another small, helpless squeak. An unwary pedestrian directed some very strong words at Maddie, as she barely avoided running him down. With a mental shake she brought her attention back to the matter at hand. Plenty of time to daydream with Allie, she decided.

Allie bounded down the stairs as Maddie drew up to the house. Looking delicious in a peach walking dress, complete with a large-brimmed peach confection sitting at a dainty angle over burnished gold curls, Allie allowed Henry to hand her into the phaeton. She pursed her lips slightly as she straightened her skirt and shot Maddie a decidedly seductive glance from under her long lashes.

Maddie felt her insides go watery, and she couldn't help letting the full light of her desire shine in her eyes. With a little cough she turned her attention to the road and gave her team office to start.

During the trip to the park, Allie went on endlessly about the weather and every other bit of inane news she could think of, causing Henry to shift uncomfortably behind them. He offered not one word of dissension when Maddie set him down at the gates of the park to await their departure. Maddie didn't require his chaperonage in the park, and he was grateful to escape Allie's pitter-patter.

"Oh, Allie! That was too bad of you! You almost bent *my* ear with all that drivel!"

"But it works every time! Instead of spending an hour at the gate arguing about whether you would require his services, your groom was exceedingly ready to see us part company with him."

"If you do it too often he'll probably look for another place of employment. I dare say your poor aunt has a terrible problem keeping good grooms around!"

"I think they've all figured it out and are really very good about leaving me my privacy. My aunt pays a good wage, so I remain quite spoiled! Don't worry, Maddie, when we escape together I'll be religiously circumspect!"

"That's going to be sooner than you think, Allie!"

"You were successful with the rich man?"

"Wonderfully so! I thought the lieutenant's man had gone past with four outriders, but the carriage behind them contained the old gentleman carrying more wealth than you can imagine! The purse I took was full of precious jewels, Allie, more than we'll ever need!"

Allie's eyes were large emerald saucers above the white gloved hand she had thrown across her mouth. "Oh Maddie," she said breathlessly, "we can look for our place in the country!"

"Soon. There are a few problems to deal with first. Marta's

got to have time to change the jewels over to coin. It will take some time if we're to avoid suspicion."

"What else?" Allie asked in a sinking tone.

"The gentleman might be able to identify me now. I think my hood slipped back on my hair when I wrestled him to the ground.

"What?" Allie said with a small squeak.

"Only because he had taken my pistol. Things had gotten a little out of hand by then," Maddie answered offhandedly.

"I should say! Perhaps you will tell me the whole story now," Allie demanded, her voice indignant.

Maddie sighed. "It was an easy hold-up when I started, but the lord had a swordstick and caught me off guard. Eventually, there was an opportunity for me to wrestle him to the ground, and then he suddenly stopped struggling. I was surprised, but gave it no further thought. I believe now that it may be due to my hood slipping back. He could not have missed my beautiful coiffure.

"Anyway, I stood and took one last look at my feisty noble-man. I guess I have a soft spot for those strong, proud types, so I threw him back his purse. I see now that I got the better end of the bargain!"

"Darling, I could hug you! You mad, wonderful woman. My only regret is that you may have endangered yourself. Luckily, the lieutenant is coming to take me to the theatre tonight, so maybe I can get some news. Come to the side door you entered last time, after the house is dark. I'll send Jane down to let you in."

"I'll be there, dearest, but now we have to work on teaching you to loop a rein."

Allie proved to be a quick student, and the two spent an enjoyable afternoon sitting close, with their heads together, talking about the future. Maddie took advantage of the situation to occasionally lay her hands over Allie's and, every now and then, to whisper endearments in her lover's ear.

Allie was tooling towards the gate to pick up Henry, when Alexandra Dinwiddie came bowling through the entrance. Etiquette demanded that the two equipages stop so the occupants could exchange greetings.

"Good day, Miss Dinwiddie," Allie said brightly.

Alexandra smiled broadly at Allie, reserving a cold nod for Maddie. "How are you, Countess? It's a wonderful day for driving, and I see you have a beautiful pair."

"Oh, they're Miss Elverton's. She has excellent taste in horse flesh, don't you think?" Allie said, no sign of devilry on her smiling face.

"Yes, of course," Alexandra said, stiffly.

"Magdalena is teaching me to drive. My aunt thinks its quite dashing, and prophesizes that it will soon be all the rage. I think it's exciting," Allie went on blithely, apparently unaware of Alexandra's growing discomfiture.

A laundalette came through the park entrance and stopped behind Alexandra's carriage.

"Oh dear, I appear to be blocking the drive," Alexandra uttered, unable to hide her relief. "Maybe we'll be able to continue this conversation soon. Good day, Countess, Miss Elverton." With a stiff prod to her coachman with her parasol, Alexandra moved off.

"She won't have that coachman long, by the look on his face," Allie observed.

"She never does. Devilishly hard on servants, I'm afraid. But if her parents are willing to tolerate it, I don't suspect there'll be any change in her behavior in the near future. What I can't fathom is her attitude towards you! She appears to fairly dote on you!"

"Alexandra is partly in love with my title, and mostly in

love with the idea of being the object of Lt. Bridgewater's attention. I'm not sure if it's his uniform that entrances her so, or his refusal to acknowledge her existence."

"Both of which make him totally loathsome."

"Not to someone like Alexandra. I suppose to her it makes him the figure of romance."

Maddie snorted in disgust but said nothing further. Henry was duly picked up and the reins returned to Maddie for the bustling trip home. Maddie sat Allie down with a meaningful goodbye and took herself home for tea with Aunt Agatha.

† † † † †

Maddie was a bundle of nerves as she waited to knock on the side door of the marchioness's town house. The last light had just gone out, and she was waiting for the house to lapse into sleep.

She had pleaded a headache to her aunt that evening, leaving Lady Elverton to attend Lady Anne's recital on her own. Circumventing Marta had not been so easy. She had become convinced that Maddie was having an affair with some undesirable male of low order, and no manner of argument could convince her otherwise. In the end Maddie had thrown up her hands.

"I'm going to see another woman, Marta. I'll be spending most of the night there," Maddie added significantly.

Marta stared at her blankly as she tried to assimilate the knowledge. "You won't be compromising your virtue then?" she asked weakly.

Maddie gave her a hearty hug. "I'll still be totally marriageable, and I'm being very, very discreet."

Marta gave a tiny smile, and a little of her colour returned.

As Maddie had known, the most important thing in Marta's eyes was that Maddie remain "undamaged" in the eyes of society. Everything else was secondary. Still, Maddie had beat a hasty retreat, just in case Marta changed her mind. She would see Marta after that intrepid woman had a night to ponder her words. Until then the night was for her and her beautiful lover.

Unable to wait any longer, Maddie gave a gentle rap on the door, which opened immediately. Jane, Allie's maid, silently led her up to Allie's door and then discreetly withdrew.

Maddie pulled the door shut behind her and gloried in the sight of her beloved. Allie stretched luxuriously on the bed, the glow from the fireplace making her rich skin seem alive with fire. Maddie drew short breaths as desire burned hot within her. In quiet grace, she slipped her clothes from her already over-warm body and moved slowly towards the bed, reveling in the dark, desirous light in Allie's shifting green eyes.

With agonizing slowness she lowered her lips to Allie's. The heat seared her as their kiss became deeper. Allie reached up with her silky arms and pulled Maddie down on top of her. Maddie's excitement grew at the feel of her lover's skin, so intimately close to hers. Her kisses rained on Allie's upturned face, and she began to nibble and kiss the beautifully exposed neck.

Her attention drifted up to Allie's ear, which she delicately traced with the tip of her tongue. Allie's breathing deepened as Maddie's hands trailed down her sides and lingered lovingly on her thighs. Allie felt a thrill of excitement as those hands returned to run their palms over excited nipples. She arched up in response and shivered with pent-up desire as Maddie's mouth covered one, then the other.

Maddie's trail of kisses moved lower across Allie's soft belly. Her tongue found her, and Allie buried her hands in Maddie's thick hair. They lay locked in mutual ecstasy, until Allie's smothered scream brought Maddie to a stop. A faint gleam of sweat on Allie's body caught the light from the fire, and Maddie lay breathless and content on Allie's thigh.

For a time they slept, happy and exhausted. Allie awoke first and smiled at her sleeping love. She lovingly caressed the dark head until Maddie's eyes slowly opened. Maddie turned her smiling face up and kissed the hand that had so gently awakened her. She crawled up next to Allie, and the two lay together, kissing and murmuring. The fires rekindled in Maddie as Allie's hands passed lightly over her skin, and the two were soon caught up in the dance of love.

Much later, when both were sated and drowsy, they lay together talking, making wonderful dreamy plans for the future.

"Maddie?"

"Hmm?"

"I talked to the lieutenant tonight."

"Good news, I hope."

"I think so, even though it was hard to discern his meaning through all the ranting and raving. By some bizarre calculation, in which your late arrival, and apparently Alexandra Dinwiddie's quiet evening at home, has somehow played a part, the lieutenant has decided that the thief is either you or Alexandra.

Maddie lay back on the bed with a groan. "I thought you said this was good news!"

"It is! The gentleman whom you held up said he thought your hair was light brown or maybe blonde. He couldn't be sure."

"But there is no way he could have missed my dark hair!"

"Whatever. The fact is that this latest clue has swung the lieutenant's suspicions towards Miss Dinwiddie."

"But he's not convinced?"

"No, not yet, of course. He'll have to be very sure of himself before he dares to act on his hunch."

"In the meantime, I have to hope nothing arouses more suspicion about me. Thank goodness, Christmas is almost upon us. His investigation will have to wait until the nobility returns to

London. Do you think we can finagle your aunt into inviting us to join you?"

"It's already done! Over tea today, out of the blue, Aunt Constance asked about your plans for the holidays. She became settled in her mind that you should travel down with us, and has set her resolve on calling on your aunt tomorrow to arrange the whole!"

"I'm beginning to sense a kindred spirit between both our aunts. There's something just a slight bit ruthless, and unstoppable, in those very determined women."

"Oh yes, but always with the very best intentions."

"Yes," Maddie said slowly, her voice heavy with thought. "I've been discovering the extent of Aunt Agatha's softness under the iron-hard shell. I think, sometimes, that underneath Aunt Agatha is really a basically shy person, not prone to trusting very easily."

"She seems to have a strong sense of loyalty."

"She certainly has stood by me! I hope that we can retire from London quietly, to avoid hurting her. There has to be a way to circumvent her pride, and set her up with her own independence. I don't believe she has a feather to fly with anymore."

"Well, worry about it later. Maybe you can invent another rich relative who timely passes away. However, if she's anything like Aunt Constance, she can list every member of the family, and their entire branch, all the way back to William the Conqueror!"

Maddie sighed, "I'm afraid so."

"We'll think of something. We've come this far."

Eight

As promised, Allie and her aunt called the next morning to invite Maddie and Lady Elverton to the marchioness's small estate. Maddie was sitting in the drawing room with her aunt, impatiently awaiting Allie's arrival, when the ladies were announced. Her aunt calmly set aside her embroidery and rose elegantly to greet Lady Sifton and Allie as they entered the sunny room.

Lady Constance warmly grasped both of Lady Agatha's hands and drew her over to the settee. She sat pertly on the edge of that elegant piece of furniture and, almost offhandedly, issued her gracious invitation.

Maddie was waiting for her aunt to reply graciously in the affirmative, and was surprised when Lady Elverton sunk to the settee among a confusion of tangled excuses. She was even more startled when Lady Sifton shifted and caught one of Lady Agatha's fluttering hands between both of her own.

"Agatha," Lady Constance murmured, quieting Lady Elverton with her soothing tone. "Aggie, I'm sorry about all the unhappiness between us in the past. Let's put it all behind us for now. For the sake of our nieces, come to Elmhurst."

"Is it truly necessary?" Lady Elverton asked reluctantly.

"It would be for the best."

Lady Agatha drew a long breath and sat erect. With calm dignity she extracted her hand from Lady Constance's.

"Magdalena and I will be happy to join you at Elmhurst," Lady Agatha stated, once more in control of herself and of the situation.

"Wonderful!" Lady Constance exclaimed, with a delighted clap of her hands. "It was my intention that Allie and I would depart tomorrow, so we could prepare for your arrival. How soon can we expect you to follow?"

"I believe that we could have everything in order in a week. It will be good to have Magdalena away from town for a rest. She's looking dreadfully pulled, don't you think?" The strain between the two aunts was gone and the conversation dissolved into a discussion of the healthiness of clean country air. Eventually, plans for the journey to Elmhurst were finalized. Allie stole a moment to lift a questioning eye at Maddie, who answered with a shrug, communicating her own bafflement.

Finished with her errand, Lady Sifton rose to depart. There was an air of briskness about her as she made her farewells. Allie's movements were much more sluggish as she and Maddie exchanged reluctant goodbyes. Both knew that the intervening week would pass with agonizing slowness.

As soon as the two ladies had left, Maddie turned to her aunt, her eyes filled with questions. She was consumed with curiosity about the cryptic dialogue between the two aunts.

Aunt Agatha proved illusive, however, and excused herself with some vague remark about speaking to the cook about dinner. Maddie was left confused and frustrated.

† † † † †

The interminable week had finally passed, and Maddie sat impatiently in the carriage, willing it to go faster. They were on the last leg of their journey now, the previous night having been spent in a well-established inn. Maddie had been all for traveling straight through to their destination, but Aunt Agatha's strongly developed sense of etiquette demanded that they travel at a decorous pace. An extra day would allow them to arrive in good time, so they would have the opportunity to rest and change before dinner.

Maddie shifted irritably in her seat. She stared blankly out the window, her eyes traveling far past the immediate landscape. Her forefinger marked a place in a novel she found impossible to read. The entire trip had been filled with visions of Allie: her face, her laughter, her love. Maddie's heart ached to be near her darling once more. Even now her mind was full of her first glimpse of Allie, her beautiful face above her elegant fan. Those deep green pools...

With a long sigh, she drew her thoughts back from that path. She had already spent too many frustrating nights thinking of Allie's cool fingers on her burning skin. Tonight, she thought with joy, she would feel those hands again.

Maddie glanced up to see her aunt staring at her with an unfathomable look on her face. A look that contained so many emotions, overlaid with a deep, deep sorrow. Without a word, and without really knowing why, Maddie reached over and held her aunt's hand. They rode the rest of the trip that way, without a word between them.

Both women were grateful when the coach finally passed through the gates of Elmhurst. They traveled up the white stone drive to the massive doors of the magnificent estate house. Allie and Lady Constance were waiting in the doorway as Maddie and Lady Agatha wearily climbed the stairs.

"Welcome to Elmhurst, Agatha, Magdalena," Lady Constance said, her formal words sitting oddly on her laughter-filled face. "Your rooms are ready. Allie, please show Magdalena her room. Agatha, if you will come with me, you'll find that your maid has not been idle since her arrival earlier."

The ladies made their way up the wide staircase. Allie led Maddie to the left, explaining, "Aunt Constance felt you and your aunt would be more comfortable arranged here in rooms across from each other. Aunt Constance and I have chambers at the other end of the hall."

Allie opened the door on a beautifully appointed bed chamber with a warm fire already blazing in the fireplace. Marta was there, efficiently unpacking, and setting the room to her satisfaction.

Allie stood in the doorway smiling, as Maddie entered. "I'll be back to make sure you have everything," she said warmly, before abandoning Maddie to Marta.

Maddie let Marta undress her and bundle her into bed. Maddie would only have an hour to rest, Marta warned, before she returned to dress her for dinner. Lady Sifton believed in keeping early hours. Country hours, Marta called them, her voice somewhere between scorn and envy, as she bustled off to press Maddie's dining gown.

The door had hardly closed behind her when a soft knock was sounded, and Allie slipped into the room. Maddie sat up and stretched out her arms as Allie flew across the floor to her.

"Darling, it's been so long!" Allie sighed into the ruffles of Maddie's nightdress. Maddie drew Allie onto the bed beside her and covered her face with kisses. It was many long minutes before any coherent words could be formed, although it's doubtful either party was aware of this.

Allie rested on Maddie's shoulder, the two exchanging details of the happenings while they had been apart. In this manner a very enjoyable hour passed.

Allie was about to leave when Marta entered, startling both Allie and Maddie. Marta gave Allie a long hard look as Allie brushed gracefully past her. She maintained her silence until Allie was gone, much to Maddie's relief.

"That's her, then?" Marta asked in a dull, resigned voice.

"Yes, Marta. Allie is my late-night rendezvous, and I don't want to hear anymore about it. If you're not satisfied, I'll understand your decision to leave."

"Miss Maddie, I raised you since you were a little babe, and I've suffered through many a queer start with you. I'll not be getting all moral on you now. Not after I've been helping you in your pursuit of crime all these years! I guess, in your own way, you know what's right for you."

Maddie bounced out of bed and gave Marta a boisterous hug. "Congratulate me then, because the most beautiful woman in the world has agreed to live with me! For the first time in my life, I am really and truly happy!"

"Yes, and you're going to be truly late, if you don't sit down here and let me do your hair."

Marta worked quickly arranging Maddie's hair, and she had just dropped Maddie's simple gown over her head when a bell rang.

"The ten-minute bell, Miss Maddie," Marta stated, struggling to fasten the snug dress.

"You've never failed to have me ready before, Marta, even though you always worry about it!"

Marta gave a noncommittal "hhrrumph" and kept her head bent to her work.

As predicted, Maddie was elegantly turned out in time to

join Lady Agatha and Lady Constance in the drawing room. Allie arrived breathlessly a few minutes later, and the ladies removed to the dining room.

The leaves had been removed from the large table to allow for a more intimate meal, and it was a lively dinner, filled with spirited conversation. Lady Constance kept the younger members of the party in stitches with her insightful stories of the *ton;* even Aunt Agatha had a sparkle in her eye as she and Lady Constance exchanged remembrances of the glorious days of their youth.

Maddie could almost see the white powdered wigs and wide panniers of that bygone age, as Lady Elverton wove story after story. Maddie had never seen her aunt so relaxed, or heard her wax so elegant before. She was charmed by her aunt's laughter and decided that Aunt Agatha must have been quite the rage in her youth, with her sparkling eyes and tripping laughter. Maddie's respect and love for her aunt deepened.

The warmth from dinner carried over to the drawing room, where Allie and Maddie took their aunts on at cards. The game was played with mock seriousness, with both pairs evenly matched. Surprisingly, it was Aunt Agatha who was the reckless and bold partner, with Lady Constance playing a conservative hand. Allie and Maddie took wild chances and spent their time, more often than not, causing the whole table to dissolve into giggles.

The clock was striking eleven before the party broke up, with Aunt Constance exclaiming with dismay at the late hour. All four ladies climbed the stairs and bade each other good night when they had reached the long hall.

The house quickly became quiet, and no one heard Allie slip down the hall to Maddie's chamber.

† † † † †

The days that followed flew by, to the dismay of everyone concerned. Allie and Maddie spent delicious afternoons walking in the crisp wind, sewing samplers together on the settee, or sitting at the spinet, playing and singing and laughing.

Lady Sifton and Lady Elverton were often seen with their heads together discussing all matters of important things. Their fondness for each other grew daily, and Aunt Agatha was the happiest Maddie had ever seen her. Gone was the stern frown and the unhappy eyes, replaced now with an undauntable smile.

The ladies occasionally entertained members of local nobility and ventured out to call on neighbors, but more often than not the evenings were spent quietly at home, and Maddie treasured those wonderful moments. As the time passed, the guarded reserve each lady kept up for society began to dissolve, and the foursome was solidified by the atmosphere of trust and intimacy.

Often Allie and Maddie would talk to each other about their feelings of security and would waver back and forth about revealing their relationship to their aunts. Always in the end they drew back from shattering the happiness and inviting their relatives' anger and disgust. It was the only discordant note in their enjoyment.

It was this same subject that they had been discussing on a long, brisk, wintery walk. Allie's nose was pink from the cold as the two slipped into the library from a side door. Their plans for a quiet interlude vanished as Allie drew a sharp breath, her muff falling to the floor as she stared with wordless surprise. Maddie turned from shutting the door to see Lady Constance leap up from her cozy position on Lady Elverton's lap.

After an uncomfortable moment, Maddie moved forward to draw Allie to her side. She smiled broadly as she stood, her arm lovingly encircling Allie's waist. Lady Constance recovered first and indulged in a happy chortle.

"You know, Aggie, we always were getting caught. I don't know why we should think that our age had made us anymore discreet!"

Lady Agatha's blush retreated at Lady Sifton's words. "Do you remember when the maid caught us, and we told her we were trying to get rid of some crumbs that had managed to fall into your bodice?" Aunt Agatha said with a chuckle, rising to stand beside Lady Constance.

"You mean you two have been lovers all these years?" Maddie exclaimed.

"No," Lady Elverton said with deep sadness. She looked questioningly at Lady Constance, who gave a slow nod.

"They might as well know the whole, Agatha. I'm tired of hiding, and it would be so nice to have friends that we can speak openly with."

Lady Elverton sighed wearily. "It has been a long time." She turned her attention back to Maddie and Allie and began to explain. "I knew Constance from an early age. Our fathers traveled in the same circles and had become friends. She came to visit for a year before our come out. One glorious, beautiful year. We became lovers, and were rarely apart.

"Then, one day, my father caught us kissing in the drawing room and raised the roof with his fury. Constance's father was called, and they stood for hours berating us. In the end they decided that marriage would be the only answer, and Constance was taken home. I was sent to my room for two weeks, until they brought me the news that Constance was engaged to be married. I tried desperately to kill myself, and almost succeeded in starving myself to death.

"Poor darling," Lady Constance murmured, as she moved to rest her head in the crook of Lady Agatha's shoulder, her arms encircling the waist of that proud lady. "My father had told me that Agatha was already married to some local squire, and so I agreed to marry the Earl of Quinton in order to put my sorrow and all the memory of Agatha behind me. It wasn't until the wedding band was securely on my finger that I discovered that my father had lied. I was going to go to her, but I felt that Agatha would never forgive me after she had held out so loyally. I was comfortable in my marriage, but never truly happy," Lady Constance ended sadly.

"In time I, too, married," continued Lady Agatha. "But my husband was a selfish oaf, and my wedded years were interminable agony. There was no word from Constance, and many times I regretted my lack of resolve to put a period to my existence. Occasionally I would read about the Marchioness of Quinton in the periodicals, but I was too bitter to try to contact her. I buried myself in the country and became a sour woman, old before my time. The death of my husband brought no relief, and I was waiting for age to do what I could not.

"Then you wrote, Maddie, and I felt a glimmer of hope that maybe your need of me might snap me out of my misery. I'm afraid that I had been unhappy for so long that I barely knew how to respond to your fresh, open friendliness. But in time I began to become deeply attached to you, and went in dread of being alone again when you married.

"I almost fainted straight away when Constance and Allie called. I'm afraid, Allie, that I didn't take much notice of you then. My eyes were all for Constance, and I had mixed feelings of anger and joy at seeing her face, so beautifully aged with all those magnificent laugh lines." She turned and softly kissed Constance's lips.

"Yes, and I tried to contact you time and time again, but you refused to answer," Constance added.

"I was hurt, and much too afraid to reopen all those old feelings, only to be rejected again."

"Maddie and Allie, you had already discovered each other, and your love was painfully obvious to one who had already experienced the same joy. I watched your love grow, until I was sure you were ready to risk all for each other," Lady Constance said.

"I watched with amusement and a little concern, Allie, as you smuggled Maddie up to your room. That was when I decided we must retire from London in order to save both of you from scandal. Long before Maddie's second visit, I was making plans to remove you from London, and I had desperately written once more to Agatha, who finally answered."

"Even the day you called to invite us down for Christmas I was still unconvinced, and dreaded Maddie experiencing the pain that I had felt."

"Yes, dearest, and you were so adorably flustered, I wanted to hold you and kiss those wonderful lips!" Lady Constance said, receiving a ferocious hug from her love.

"So we moved to Elmhurst," Constance continued, "and you two were so enraptured by each other that it was easy to woo my lady love. We were able to unravel our past and discover that our love had not dimmed through the years.

"In fact, we were just making plans to stay here with each other, far away from London, and I have Agatha's approval in inviting you two to stay with us, if that is what you wish," Lady Constance finished.

Allie squealed with joy and swung Maddie around. Her initial exuberance was dimmed, however, as Maddie stood rigidly.

"I'm afraid we cannot accept your very generous offer, Lady Sifton," Maddie said, ignoring Allie's dismay.

Lady Constance laughed at Maddie's stiff pride. "My dear, your aunt has known for some time about your nocturnal activities, although it is only recently that she concluded that it involved highway robbery. Did you think two women like us, who have gone against society since our youth, would throw up our hands in horror at your thievery? Personally, my dear, I think it's quite romantic and very, very dashing!"

Maddie turned to her aunt. "You knew all this and you didn't say anything?"

"What could I say, Maddie? I had no money to take care of you," Aunt Agatha said tenderly. "At the time it seemed to be the only answer."

Maddie moved to a large leather armchair and slumped there despairingly.

"I can't believe I've been so transparent! All of you have figured me out so easily, how can I hope that I've fooled Lt. Bridgewater? It's only a matter of time before he solves the puzzle." Maddie opened her hands in a hopeless gesture.

"But he suspects Alexandra, love. Surely that is a point in your favor. Besides, the lieutenant cannot be as boldly intelligent and intuitive as the four of us!" Allie said helpfully, plopping herself down on Maddie's lap.

Lady Agatha sank onto the settee, pulling Lady Constance down beside her. She leaned forward as she spoke. "Perhaps you should explain to me who exactly Lt. Bridgewater is, and how much he knows about you."

Maddie gave a tired smile and then began a long oration of everything that had transpired since the lieutenant, through Allie, had entered her life. Allie interjected her own thoughts and observations as Maddie spoke, and the aunts remained silent, except for a small squeak from Lady Constance when Maddie mentioned the jewels she had confiscated.

No one spoke when Maddie finished, and there was a long period of silence as each lady remained engrossed in her own thoughts.

Lady Constance was the first to speak. "The handling of the

jewels is easy enough. I have a very comfortable income that I draw from the estate. It is enough to keep us in graceful style, and as long as the land produces, our security here is guaranteed. Your very capable butler will be able to travel to London regularly, to supply us with a steady flow of income from the jewels. It will provide for the amenities such as trips to town, if any of us should get the urge."

Maddie snorted and Allie crinkled her pretty nose.

"Or a fine pair for your carriage," Lady Constance continued with a smile. "I'm afraid, however, that the lieutenant has me totally baffled."

"It should not be too difficult to turn the lieutenant's suspicions to our favor," Aunt Agatha broke in, her voice rich with satisfaction. "I think, Constance, that you should hold a ball when we return to London."

"Of course! It would be a pleasure. Shall I invite the lieutenant?"

"And I think Alexandra and her parents, Lord and Lady Winifer," Agatha said with a nod. "And perhaps that foolish viscount and Lord Edmund, so Maddie and Allie will have someone pliable to dance with. Let me explain the wonderful scene we are going to create."

Lady Agatha's magnificent yet very simple plan was unfolded, to the delight of all the participants. Maddie found her spirits returning as she began to see the light at the end of the tunnel.

Lady Constance clapped her hands in glee. "When shall we set the date for the ball, then?"

"I think we should return with the first arrivals in London after the holidays. We should be able to hold a small ball a week later," Agatha said decisively.

"A week! Agatha, you must be overheated! How can I arrange such a large event in just a week? With everything that has to be done, invitations sent, decorations ordered, it can't be done. My cook would leave! And rightly so! And how can I decide if. . ."

"Connie." Aunt Agatha held the marchioness's flustered face between her hands. Gently she kissed Lady Constance's forehead. "It *can* be done. You have two energetic young ladies to help you with such niceties as invitations, and a bevy of servants that can be sent to London with your instructions. We will start now, and there will be plenty of time to get everything in order."

"Besides, Aunt Constance," Allie added, "everyone knows how important it is to be seen at one of your gatherings. I daresay you'll be responsible for an early migration back to town!"

"Yes, of course. I'm being silly. I've never let small details overwhelm me in the past, and I see no reason why they should now. But be forewarned, Agatha, you're going to have to roll up your sleeves and join in!"

"It will be my pleasure! Our first ball together. Perhaps a Seven Day Wonder! Allie," Agatha turned her attention from her lover, "I think it would be wise if you sent the invitation to Lt. Bridgewater. You will want him to escort you to the affair, and we will count on him arriving in London early to arrange a heavy guard of the main postroads. Perhaps it will offer you the opportunity to speak with him on his return, judge his position, and discreetly fire his suspicions of Alexandra."

There was a sense of agreement and completeness among the ladies. They chatted for awhile about plans for the ball, each content and looking forward to the holiday festivities with genuine delight. Eventually the party broke up to dress for dinner.

Allie and Maddie went out on each other's arm, laughing and joking. Lady Constance moved to follow, but Lady Agatha held her back. They kissed deeply for a moment.

"I love you so much, Constance," Lady Agatha sighed.

"This has been the greatest time of my life. I don't ever want it to end."

"It shan't, precious," Lady Constance answered, kissing Lady Agatha passionately. "As long as you never ask me to hold a last-minute engagement again." The last was added with a mischievous gleam, and Lady Constance raced out of the room with a small squeal as Lady Agatha reached for her waist.

Nine

When the ladies finally made their way back to London, all were content and happy and looking forward to the time when they could return to the serenity of Elmhurst.

Maddie smiled down at Allie, who had drifted off to sleep as the carriage rocked them softly. How different the return trip was from the agonizing journey from London. She felt peaceful and relaxed as she rode with one arm around her lady love.

Across from Maddie, Lady Agatha and Lady Constance rode with their eyes closed, their hands resting in each other's. Maddie studied her aunt's face, torn between hope and doubt that that intrepid lady had found a way of escape for her. Her arm tightened around Allie, causing her to stir in her sleep. No matter what, she would find a way to spend her life with her beloved.

Maddie rested her head back and watched the miles pass. A happy expression settled on her face as her mind traveled back over the past weeks. Never in her wildest imagination had she thought that life could be as wonderful as it had been at Elmhurst.

She had spent so many wonderful hours with Allie, safe and confident that they would now have a place in the world. Together they had tackled the invitations for the massive guest list Aunt Constance had compiled, and they had watched with some dismay as Lady Sifton managed to turn the entire household on its ear by her long and urgent requests.

Messengers had flown off to London nearly every day to complete errands for Lady Constance, and Maddie and Allie had awaited breathlessly to see what the outcome of the brouhaha would be.

Lady Agatha had maintained her serenity through it all, and had proved to be the most successful liaison between Lady Constance and her frantic staff. Lady Elverton's calm demeanor could soothe the most ruffled feathers, and was likely the reason that the cook and many other valued retainers decided to remain in the marchioness's employ.

In the final week before Christmas many of the details of the ball had been resolved, and Aunt Agatha had taken it upon herself to call a halt to the whole proceeding.

Peace settled upon the estate, and the four ladies had enjoyed a marvelous Christmas. Maddie and Allie had reveled in their new freedom of being able to express their affections physically with each other, and Lady Agatha had to more than once remind them of the need for discreetness around the servants.

Maddie smiled to herself, holding the happy thoughts

around her until the gentle motion of the carriage overcame her and she drifted asleep.

It wasn't until the sounds of London reached her that Maddie awoke. The coach was traveling directly to the Elverton's town house where Lady Agatha had proposed that they gather for their evening repast. Lady Constance was prepared to travel home afterwards but, after much pleading, Allie was being allowed to spend the night. The young ladies could be fitted for their ball gowns at the same time, Lady Elverton had argued, siding with Maddie and Allie.

The ladies climbed wearily out of the coach and made their way indoors. Lady Constance and Allie were escorted to rooms where they could freshen up and change for the dinner Marta had masterfully arranged upon her arrival earlier. They gladly excused themselves to clean off the grime from traveling, and Aunt Constance looked longingly at the bed as the dinner chime sounded.

The dinner was an enjoyable but brief affair, without the usual spate of lively conversation. Everyone was feeling tired and jarred, and they were eager to retire to the privacy of the drawing room.

They sat in the glow of the fire and discussed at some length what final preparations were needed before the marchioness's ball. There was a reluctance among the group to leave the warmth of their budding friendship to face society once more. Each felt a sense of camaraderie that gave them the strength to make this final splash in the *ton*. Still, there was no urgency among the ladies to break up for the evening.

At last Lady Constance rose to return home, eager to reach her bed. Maddie and Allie withdrew from the drawing room to allow their aunts privacy for their goodbyes. Later, long after Maddie and Allie had slipped into bed together, the drawing room opened again, and Maddie and Allie exchanged sly smiles with each other before disappearing under the covers.

† † † † †

Several days after the ladies had returned to London, Lt. Bridgewater called on Allie. She burst into laughter as she recounted the story to Maddie.

"He really has an active imagination," Allie said as the two sat on the settee. "He's full of plans and schemes. Traps for the highwayman on the road, traps for the thief if she should decide to attend my aunt's ball. Indeed, I will be very grateful when all of this is over. He grows more outrageous every day with this obsession."

"Did you speak to him about Alexandra?" Maddie asked, her voice unable to hide the urgency she felt.

"Of course, silly! It was easy to encourage him to elaborate. Alexandra has become the focal point of his suspicions, and every action of hers becomes suspect. He almost convinced himself that it was his duty to clap her up on the spot!"

"I take it you were able to change his mind?"

"A few well-placed words about Lord Winifer's position and his numerous political contacts managed to cool the lieutenant's passions for awhile. I suggested to him that we should use the ball as the setting for gathering more decisive information of Alexandra's guilt.

"I offered my help in keeping an eye on Alexandra, and he had taken it upon himself to call on her tomorrow. I believe he intends to ask her to put him down on her card for a waltz. I was amazed."

"It's too bad for Alexandra, though. She really believes she has developed a *tendre* for the lieutenant," Maddie said sadly.

"She will see him in his true colours at the ball. She will be hurt, and perhaps embarrassed, but her father's considerable influence will protect her from any lasting damage. Why all this sudden concern for Alexandra?" Allie asked, her brow wrinkled with confusion. "I thought the two of you could barely be civil to each other."

"Perhaps it's because now that I'm free to love the most wonderful woman in the world, I can see how truly unhappy Alexandra is. She doesn't need me to add to her unhappiness."

Allie rewarded Maddie with a long kiss, which both were reluctant to have end. Maddie had a final fitting for her gown, however, and soon rose to leave. Maddie gave Allie a final kiss goodbye with a whispered promise to visit her that night, and left Allie to deal with the footman, who wanted to know where the potted plants were to go.

† † † † †

Maddie sat impatiently drumming her fingers on the arm of her chair. She stared blankly at the darkness outside her window wondering how Allie was doing. She conjured up a vision of Allie in the receiving line at Lady Sifton's ball.

Undoubtedly it would be a huge success, and by now Allie would be tiring of her duties as hostess. Maddie smiled as she imagined Allie shifting her tired feet as another guest was passed to her from her aunt. She would be thinking of sitting to rest her feet, but would be too excited to actually do so.

At least Allie had something to distract her, Maddie thought as she stood to take a couple of brisk laps around the room. She, on the other hand, was as frustrated as a caged lion.

The day had seemed interminable as she and Lady Elverton had spent the time quietly at home. Her aunt had sat coolly stitching, as Maddie had repeatedly put down her book to study the clock on the mantle. Time and again Maddie had jumped up to stride to the window, remarking to her aunt how slowly time was passing.

Always her aunt had given an offhand response, unperturbed by Maddie's gyrations. It was only after they had finished their evening repast and had once again retired to the sitting

126

room that Aunt Agatha finally lost her patience with Maddie. With some stern words about Maddie's behavior, her aunt had suggested that they both withdraw to their rooms to rest.

Maddie chuckled softly. Her aunt, of course, had withdrawn to remove herself from Maddie's tiring restlessness. Both ladies were well aware that rest was the farthest thing from Maddie's mind.

Maddie took another turn about her room before stopping to rest her heated forehead on the cool pane of glass. If only the night was over! Maddie sighed. How much longer must she wait?

The door clicked open behind her as Marta bustled into the room. Maddie whirled around and bounced over to the dressing table, impatient to begin dressing for the ball. Marta stared silently for a moment, her arms akimbo, but in the end decided that comment would be wasted and silently began dressing Maddie's hair.

"Miss Maddie, sit still!" Marta chided as Maddie shifted in her chair. "You've been a nervous wreck all day. The more you fidget the longer it's going to take me, so you might as well relax."

"I'm sorry, Marta. I'm just so nervous! Tonight is so important, and I keep thinking what if we make a mistake? What if the whole thing goes the wrong way and the lieutenant arrests me?"

"Is that what you are stewing about? Now listen here, young lady," Marta said sternly. "Everyone knows that if you think bad thoughts then that is surely what is going to happen. Now you sit there and think happy thoughts while I finish getting you ready."

"But, I . . ."

"No time for weak 'buts.' You do as I say. Takes a little more work to think good thoughts, but you'll be glad you did."

Maddie said nothing further, her concentration now on the

perfect execution of their plan. Marta finished her hair and moved to drop the elegant ball gown over Maddie's head.

Lacing up Maddie's dress, Marta smiled at Maddie's reflection in the long mirror.

"Thinking happy thoughts isn't supposed to crease your forehead, Miss Maddie," was the only comment Marta made.

At last Maddie was ready to join her aunt. She entered the drawing room, where Lady Elverton was waiting, and made a small sound of dismay at seeing her aunt quietly stitching a handkerchief.

"Aunt Agatha, isn't it time to leave?" Maddie asked anxiously.

"In a minute, Magdalena," her aunt answered, without lifting her head from her work.

Maddie slumped sullenly in a chair. "But you've been sewing all day!"

"This last piece of work is very important."

Maddie said nothing as she watched her aunt place her careful stitches. In less time than Maddie had imagined, Lady Elverton cut her thread and spread the handkerchief out on her knee.

Maddie leaned forward to view the material more closely. "Aunt Agatha," she gasped. "How shrewd of you!"

She picked up the handkerchief to admire the initials stitched there. Maddie traced her finger over them. "A.D.," they read. Alexandra Dinwiddie: the last piece of "evidence" they needed to cause the lieutenant's misstep. Maddie put her arm through her aunt's as the estimable lady tucked the handkerchief neatly away in her reticule. Together they made their way to the waiting coach.

† † † † †

The ladies entered the ballroom on cue, at precisely ten o'clock. Lady Elverton was warmly greeted by Lady Constance, as Maddie stole a minute to search the room for Allie.

Like a magnet, Maddie's eyes locked on Allie almost immediately. There was her beloved across the room, on Lord Edmund's arm, speaking to Alexandra. From the bemused look on Lord Edmund's face, Maddie was sure that Allie had used some high-handed tactics to get him there.

Allie looked up and caught Maddie's eye. Maddie dropped a quick wink, which Allie answered with a little smile before returning her attention to Alexandra.

Maddie watched as Allie ended her conversation with Miss Dinwiddie and began to move off with Lord Edmund. As Allie brushed past Alexandra she executed a gracious twist that resulted in a small trip. The loud rip that resulted informed Allie that her well-aimed step had landed on the ruffled hem of Alexandra's dress.

Immediately Allie dissolved into a confusion of apologies, which Miss Dinwiddie graciously brushed aside, despite the evident dismay she was feeling. All flustered concern, Allie led Alexandra off to a small, curtained alcove, in order to tack up the errant ruffle.

Maddie hid her smile at her lover's delightful drama and turned her attention back to the situation at hand. She stood demurely by her aunt as Lady Elverton drew Lady Sifton aside for an intense conversation.

From the corner of her eye, Maddie scanned the room for Lt. Bridgewater. She finally located him craning his head about, obviously in search of someone. Maddie hoped it was Alexandra he was looking for.

She closed her eyes, willing him to approach Lady Constance for guidance in finding the young lady. She imagined him approaching and was quite startled when she heard a male voice address the marchioness.

"Lady Sifton, may I interrupt to enquire the whereabouts of the countess? I believe I have this dance."

Maddie's eyes flew open to focus on the lieutenant standing

rigidly before Lady Constance. For a brief moment Maddie's mind flew back to her conversation with Marta, but she impatiently dismissed the thought.

"Allie's whereabouts are not important right now. Lady Elverton has related some startling information to me that I think you must hear. Perhaps we can retire to one of the alcoves for a little more privacy." Lady Sifton's voice brooked no refusal, and she firmly linked arms with the lieutenant and drew him away.

Lady Elverton and Maddie moved to follow, and Maddie shot a glance across the room to where Alexandra was ensconced. She watched Allie appear from behind the curtain and move in the direction of Alexandra's esteemed mama, Lady Elena. Maddie felt a surge of confidence at the neat execution of their plan as she followed Lady Agatha into the alcove.

Inside, Maddie found Lady Elverton's attention directed at Lt. Bridgewater. Lady Agatha's voice was beginning to climb as she warmed to her theme of thieves and the law, and in particular the lieutenant's apparent inability to deal with these marauders.

Maddie watched with admiration as Aunt Agatha narrowed her attack, supplying an oration on Lady Sifton's horrible attack by a nefarious robber.

"Lt. Bridgewater, I demand to know what you are going to do about these horrible criminals! Today, in broad daylight, my own carriage was held up by some thieving scoundrel."

Maddie watched the lieutenant's face as Lady Agatha's words broke in upon him. Lady Elverton remained seemingly unaware of the fire her words lit in the lieutenant's breast.

"I'm lucky not to have perished from fear," Lady Elverton continued without pause. "But I managed to remain strong to protect my dear, sweet Magdalena from the ruffian. A person's not safe to travel even by daylight anymore." Lady Elverton's tone threatened a fit of strong histrionics. Lady Sifton put a soothing arm around her shoulders and patted her hand consolingly.

"But I heard nothing of this! Did you tell anyone? Have you reported this?" The lieutenant's eyes burned with intensity.

"No. I couldn't. How could I? It was probably some young nobleman, trying to win some silly wager. He is obviously involved with a woman of quality." Aunt Agatha paused dramatically, luring the lieutenant deeper into the snare.

"Yes?" Lt. Bridgewater asked, faltering under the suspense. This was Lady Agatha at her finest.

"He was sneering when he left, unaware that he had dropped *this!*" Aunt Agatha, with theatrical flourish, held forth a small white handkerchief.

She sniffed at the lieutenant's blank face. "A woman's handkerchief, Lt. Bridgewater, with the initials 'A.D.'"

Maddie almost applauded as Lady Elverton administered the *coup de grace*. There was no hope for the lieutenant now.

The lieutenant grabbed the handkerchief with unholy glee and almost danced in place. He whirled to Lady Constance.

"Where is Alexandra Dinwiddie?" he demanded.

"Alexandra?" Maddie exclaimed, in a breathless squeak.

"I saw her retire to an alcove with the countess. I believe she needed a few stitches in her dress," Lady Sifton said innocently, her voice startled.

"Undoubtedly she'll use that as an excuse to slip away!" Lady Agatha exclaimed, firing the lieutenant's imagination.

Grasping Lady Constance by the arm, he ordered, "Take me to her immediately, Lady Sifton!"

Lady Constance suppressed an urge to drop his loathsome hand from her arm and deliver a stinging set-down for his impertinent tone. Instead she allowed him to direct her to the ballroom.

Maddie made her way from the alcove, confident that

Lady Constance would be able to suppress the lieutenant's movements to a decorous pace as he circled the dance floor to reach Alexandra.

Maddie decided to move around the floor in the opposite direction, so that she could join up smoothly with Allie. Even now Allie was drawing the stiffly correct Lady Elena in the direction of the alcove.

"Where to so quickly, Maddie?"

Maddie jumped, badly startled.

"Charles, what are you doing?" she demanded. "You could be the death of someone with your sneaky ways!"

"I wasn't sneaking, although I do admit I was spying. I saw you slip off with a very stuffy group to an alcove, and I was consumed with curiosity. I decided to lie in wait for you here and demand an explanation, but you marched right on past me. I was hurt, Magdalena."

"Totally outrageous as always, Charles. But I don't have time for your high drama. I have some business to attend to."

"As I've been observing. Let me speculate that it involves the lieutenant, Miss Dinwiddie, our hostess, and other key players."

"Not now! Let me go," Maddie demanded, her anger beginning to visibly rise.

"I'll go with you."

Maddie sighed and turned to face the viscount squarely. She placed one hand on his chest.

"Charles. You've been a dear and true friend, but there are parts of my life where you cannot follow. You must let me go." Maddie's words were soft, and both were aware that her words carried more than their surface meaning.

"Goodbye, Maddie," the viscount said sadly. He lifted her hand from his chest and gently kissed the tips of her fingers.

"Goodbye, Charles," she answered, touching his face. It

132

hurt to see the pain in his eyes, but Maddie knew this was her final break from London.

She whirled away from the viscount, her breath choppy, and focused her attention on the alcove. She was just in time to see Lt. Bridgewater enter the alcove alone.

She hurried to reach the small room, but was too late to catch any of the proceedings happening therein.

† † † † †

"Ah, ha!" said the lieutenant in dramatic tones, causing Alexandra to jump and nearly prick herself with her needle. "Now I've got you!" he exclaimed at the startled woman's face.

"Why yes, Michael, I believe you do have me. Now what?" Alexandra answered vacantly.

In her mind the lieutenant's behavior echoed all the wonderful romances she had read. Dreamily, she was imagining how the abduction would take place at such a public affair, when the lieutenant's voice startled her again.

"You are a highway robber, Alexandra! There's no use trying to escape the law now! I have proof! A little something you dropped at your last holdup! Maybe you recognize this handkerchief!"

"Michael, what are you talking about? Highway robberies and handkerchiefs. I'm sure I don't understand!"

"Don't play stupid anymore, Alexandra. I know you are a criminal mastermind."

Alexandra's continued look of embafflement infuriated him, and he stepped forward to shake her.

"Michael," Alexandra squeaked, her voice broken by his rough handling. Outside, Lady Sifton took her cue and, drawing back the curtain, proceeded to faint straight away.

Maddie and Allie raced to her side, followed by Lady Elverton and Lady Elena. One glance into the alcove revealed Lt. Bridgewater frozen in position, his hands incriminatingly locked on Alexandra's arms.

Alexandra wrenched herself away and collapsed, sobbing, into her mother's arms. The orchestra had stopped playing in their curiosity of the proceedings, and the little scenario in the alcove soon had the entire room as an audience.

Through the din, a deep voice resounded. "Alexandra, what in the blazes is going on here?"

Lady Sifton, who had made a miraculous recovery, moved to salvage the situation by laying a calming hand on Alexandra's irate parent's arm. She suggested all members involved withdraw to the library. She then led Papa firmly from the room, letting the others follow in a haphazardly fashion. Allie lifted her arm and directed the orchestra to resume playing.

When all had gathered in the library, Alexandra's father again demanded to know what had thrown his daughter into the midst of a furious scandal.

Lt. Bridgewater, his face a little pale but still quite determined, stepped forward. "Sir, your daughter is not as she appears. I have had delivered to me tonight evidence that your daughter is the infamous highway robber, who has been terrorizing London these past few years."

"What?!" Lord Winifer roared furiously.

"I have this proof," the lieutenant said, bravely extending the handkerchief, his face now chalk white.

"You are insane, sirrah, and I'll see you transferred for this!"

"Lady Elverton, tell him about being held up today!" the lieutenant ordered, despairingly.

"But, dear boy, we don't have the foggiest notion of what you are talking about! We never left London today!" Aunt Agatha said, in shocked surprise. "I believe you're right, Lord Winifer. I think he's quite insane."

"But I'm not! Lady Sifton, you were there when she told me!"

"You really are quite disillusioned. You're right, Lady El-verton, but for his family's sake I suppose we must keep him out of Bedlam. A sojourn in the country might snap him out of it."

"I'll have him transferred to South America!" Lord Winifer threatened.

"That sounds wonderful! Such a romantic-sounding place, South America. Perhaps you would find such a trip refreshing, Lt. Bridgewater?" Lady Sifton said, her voice tripping.

The lieutenant said nothing, his expression dazed.

"It is an overwhelming thought," Lady Constance continued. "Take time to think it over. So lucky to be a man, and experience so much adventure!"

"Ah, Allie, you've brought the footmen," Lady Elverton broke in smoothly, saving Lady Constance from further conversation. "Very good. Lord Winifer, I hope you can arrange to have him held until his departure. One never knows, but he may be dangerous."

"Never fear, Marchioness, I will handle it all," Lord Wini-fer said, unhappy to be caught up in the messy scandal, but hoping he and his family would be able to rise above it.

Lt. Bridgewater stood blankly in the center of the room. Beneath his dazed look his mind was working furiously, and suddenly his head snapped up.

His face twisted with rage as he spat, *"You!"* All the helpless fury was communicated in that one word, as he lunged at Maddie. His hands had barely closed around her throat, as the footmen grabbed him and wrestled him to the floor. They quickly hustled him away, screaming and cursing, his accusations traveling behind him.

Maddie sat down on the settee, her face white and her body trembling. Allie and Aunt Agatha moved to her side, and Lady Sifton escorted Lord Winifer and his family to his carriage, which Allie had called for earlier. Apologies were exchanged all around, and Lord Winifer again asserted that he would handle it all. He perfectly understood Lady Sifton's desire to withdraw from town, after having such an unhappy episode occur at her ball. Lady Constance could barely conceal her relief as the carriage moved off.

Inside, Lady Constance found Maddie with her composure restored.

"That poor man," Maddie said sadly.

"He brought it upon himself. We just brought to a head something that was eventually bound to happen. His violence was inexcusable. Indeed, I feel badly about endangering Alexandra so. The poor dear is terrified, and that dangerous man left bruise marks on her arms. Don't forget that, Maddie. Any man willing to resort to violence will find it easier to do so a second time. I, for one, am glad I will never see him again," Lady Agatha concluded, her tone resolved.

"I suppose you're right, Aunt Agatha. All that exposed rage was very disconcerting," Maddie said, lifting a hand to her throat.

"Perhaps you and Allie should retire upstairs. Agatha and I will deal with the guests," Lady Sifton said gently.

"Not without a victory toast," Lady Elverton cut in. "Poke your head out the door, Allie, and see if you can convince one of your overworked servants to bring some champagne. Do you realize, ladies, that we have done it!"

Victorious hugs were exchanged all around, and after the champagne had arrived the ladies joined in on a loud toast to their future.

It was Lady Constance who finally broke up the festive gathering.

"My guests!" she exclaimed, snapping her glass down on the desk she was gracing. "Agatha, they'll be speculating and talking by now. We owe it to Alexandra to smooth things over, to say nothing of salvaging my reputation as a hostess."

Lady Elverton laughed as she drew Lady Sifton to the door. "See, my dear, I told you it would be a Seven Day Wonder. In the future the *ton* will flock to our balls to see what will happen next!"

Maddie and Allie missed the rest of that happy speech as the two ladies exited to rejoin their guests.

After an exchange of glances, Allie and Maddie slipped up the back stairs to Allie's room, where her maid helped them both to undress. Maddie slipped into a nightdress of Allie's, and both women crawled into bed, exhausted.

They lay in silence for a long while before Maddie let out a long breath. "You know, Allie, now I've got it all!" She rolled over and covered Allie's face with kisses, her hands drifting over the thin nightdress covering Allie's body.

"Do you think we'll leave for Elmhurst tomorrow?" she asked, as she tugged at the strings holding the gown together.

"I suppose, Maddie. But believe me, at this moment it's the farthest thing from my mind."

And indeed it was, as the room became full of the sounds of passion.

Other books of interest from
ALYSON PUBLICATIONS

Don't miss our FREE BOOK offer at the end of this section.

☐ **A MISTRESS MODERATELY FAIR,** by Katherine Sturtevant. $9.00. Seventeenth-century London is not accustomed to women such as Margaret Featherstone. A widowed playwright, she manages her own affairs, and competes with some of the most talented men in the realm. But she hides a secret, a secret that actress Amy Dudley shares, and that threatens to deliver them both to the gallows.

☐ **WANDERGROUND,** by Sally Miller Gearhart, $7.00. Here are stories of the hill women, who combine the control of mind and matter with a sensuous adherence to women's realities and history. A lesbian classic.

☐ **CHOICES,** by Nancy Toder, $8.00. This popular novel about lesbian love depicts the joy, passion, conflicts and intensity of love between women as Nancy Toder conveys the fear and confusion of a woman coming to terms with her sexual and emotional attraction to other women.

☐ **TESTIMONIES: A collection of lesbian coming our stories,** edited by Sarah Holmes, $8.00. An all-new collection of stories in which women of different races and backgrounds describe the passion and conflicts of their attraction to other women.

☐ **THE CRYSTAL CURTAIN,** by Sandy Bayer, $8.00. Stephanie Nowland had felt the power, even as a child — the power to see what was hidden, to sense the future. She used the power to help others.

Now a crazed, sadistic killer wants revenge on the woman who sent him to prison. He wants to kill her lover, Marian, too. Images of both women's deaths fill his thoughts.

Stephanie can see them there.

☐ **UNBROKEN TIES: Lesbian Ex-Lovers,** by Carol Becker, Ph.D., $8.00. Lesbian relationships with ex-lovers are complex and unusual ways of building alternative families and social networks. Carol Becker's interviews with numerous pairs of ex-lovers tell the trauma of breaking-up, the stages of recovery, and the differing ways of maintaining close emotional connections with former lovers.

☐ **THE PEARL BASTARD,** by Lillian Halegua, $4.00. Frankie is fifteen when she leaves her large, suffocating Catholic family. Here, with painful innocence and acute vision, she tells the story of her sudden entry into a harsh maturity.

☐ **LIFETIME GUARANTEE,** by Alice Bloch, $7.00. Here is the personal and powerfully-written chronicle of a woman faced with the impending death of her sister from cancer, at the same time that she must also face her family's reaction to her lesbianism.

☐ **IRIS,** by Janine Veto, $7.00. When Iris and Dee meet in Hawaii, they both know that this is the relationship they have each been looking for; all they want is to live together on this island paradise forever. But the world has other plans, and Iris and Dee find that their love must now face a formidable foe if it is to survive.

☐ **BETWEEN FRIENDS,** by Gillian E. Hanscombe, $7.00. Frances and Meg were friends in school years ago; now Frances is a married housewife while Meg is a lesbian involved in progressive politics. Through letters written between these women and their friends, the author weaves an engrossing story while exploring many vital lesbian and feminist issues.

☐ **CRUSH,** by Jane Futcher, $7.00. It wasn't easy fitting in at an exclusive girls' school, but now — in her senior year — Jinx finally felt like she belonged. Even beautiful, popular Lexie wanted to be her friend. Just being near Lexie made Jinx feel dizzy and wonderful.
   But just as Jinx decided that this crush on Lexie had to end, Lexie made it clear that she had other plans . . . and Lexie always got her own way.

☐ **MACHO SLUTS,** by Pat Califia, $9.00. Califia, the prolific lesbian author whose "Adviser" column is a regular feature in the *Advocate*, has put together a stunning collection of her best erotic short fiction. She writes with skill and verve, exploring S/M fantasy and sexual adventure in taboo territory.

☐ **THE ALYSON ALMANAC,** $7.00. Almanacs have been popular sources of information since Yankee farmers started forecasting the weather. Here is a sourcebook for gay men and lesbians that offers financial planning for same-sex couples, short biographies of nearly two-hundred gay people throughout history, unusual vacation ideas, and much, much more.

☐ **LONG TIME PASSING: Lives of Older Lesbians,** by Marcy Adelman, ed., $8.00. Here, in their own words, women talk about age-related concerns: the fear of losing a lover; the experiences of being a lesbian in the 1940s and 1950s; and issues of loneliness and community.

Get this book FREE!

Sometime in the last century, two women living on the coast of France, loved each other. They had no other models for such a thing, so one of them posed as a man for most of their life together. This legend is still told in Brittany; from it, Jeannine Allard has created *Légende*, a hauntingly beautiful story of two women in love.

Normally $6.00, *Légende* is yours **free** when you order any three other books described here. Just check the box at the bottom of the order form on the next page.

☐ **DEAR SAMMY: Letters from Gertrude Stein and Alice B. Toklas,** by Samuel M. Steward, $8.00. As a young man, Samuel M. Steward journeyed to France to meet the two women he so admired. It was the beginning of a long friendship. Here he combines his fascinating memoirs of Toklas and Stein with photos and more than a hundred of their letters.

☐ **MURDER IS MURDER IS MURDER,** by Samuel M. Steward, $7.00. Gertrude Stein and Alice B. Toklas go sleuthing through the French countryside, attempting to solve the mysterious disappearance of their neighbor, the father of their handsome gardener. A new and very different treat from the author of the Phil Andros stories.

☐ **DEAD HEAT,** by Willyce Kim, $7.00. Dancer and the crew meet up for a new adventure involving Vinny 'The Skull', horse racing, and a kidnapped gypsy, but the result is one fast-paced, entertaining story you'll read again and again.

To get these books:

Ask at your favorite bookstore for the books listed here. You may also order by mail. Just fill out the coupon below, or use your own paper if you prefer not to cut up this book.

GET A FREE BOOK! When you order any three books listed here at the regular price, you may request a *free* copy of *Légende*.

— — — — — — — — — — — — — — — — —

Enclosed is $_____ for the following books. (Add $1.00 postage when ordering just one book; if you order two or more, we'll pay the postage.)

1. _____

2. _____

3. _____

4. _____

5. _____

☐ Send a free copy of *Légende* as offered above. I have ordered at least three other books.

name: _____

address: _____

city:_____ state:_____zip:_____

ALYSON PUBLICATIONS
Dept. H-51, 40 Plympton St., Boston, Mass. 02118

This offer expires Dec. 31, 1991. After that date, please write for current catalog.